WAR AND LOVE

WINTER RENSHAW

COVER DESIGN: Louisa Maggio

EDITING: Wendy Chan

PROOFREADERS: Janice Owen and Carey Sullivan

COVER MODEL: Gilberto Fritsch

PHOTOGRAPHER: Wong Sim

 Created with Vellum

IMPORTANT

DESCRIPTION

My lies? Impeccable.

My heart? Cold as ice.

My only job? To convince her what we had was as real as the diamond I was hired to place on her finger.

The battle was someone else's.

I was merely a soldier, recruited by a wealthy stranger who made it unapologetically clear that my future—and everything I've ever worked for—depended on the successful completion of this mission.

I was prepared for war.

I wasn't prepared for Love Aldridge.

This book is lovingly dedicated to the following members of
CAMP WINTER:

Alexis Alston
Alisha Woolls
Allison East
Amanda Incles
Amy Leibenguth
Angela Sinclair Haley
Anne Flammang Spencer
Ashley Blevins
Becky Carter Nichols
Bobbi Schwarz
Brandi Morrone
Bre Demko
Bridget Hobden
Caoimhe Duddy
Caroline Frimston
Catherine Finegan
Charlene Dalton
Charmaine Walker
Chrissy Blanchfield
Christa Livingstone

Christina Nazworth
Christine Buczek
Christine Godfrey
Christine Reese
Cindy Frazier
Cynthia Keech McCarty
Dana Land
Dani Nicole
Danielle Amos
Deanna Dodge
Diane Cerveny
Donna Causey
Elizette Guerrero-Lopez
Erica Westerhoff
Felicia Eddy
Grace Forte
Harloe Rae
Heather Bothern
Heather Firth
Heidi Mowry
Jackie Juane
Jackie Wang
Jacqueline Ellison
Jacquie Czech Martin
Jasmine Joyner
Jeannette Bauroth
Jen Champlin
Jenn Allen
Jennifer Marie Perez
Jennifer Matthews Sharo
Jessica Cooper
Jill Kirtley
Joan Day

Joanne Blakey
Jocelyne Germain
Kari Hansen
Karin Enders
Karine Creve-coeur
Katherine Miles
Kathy Tucker Gutierrez
Katie Anne Gentle
Kelly Johnson Homan
Kelly Latham
Keri Roth
Kristhia Seward
Kristina Morgan
Krystel Allen
Laila Viking
Larissa Berty
Laura Apodaca Gonzalez
Linda Barrett
Lindsey Wheelon
Lisa Nuyen
Lisa Stark
Lyze Gillett
Madeleine East
Mairim Santos
Mandy Mitchell
Mariah Gunter
Martinique Martinez
Melissa Hetherington
Mellissa Carlson
Michelle Mayer
Missy Carter
Misty Marie Schott
MJ Villaespin

Myla Theresa

Natalie Ruiz McLean

Nikki Brackett

Nina Piatt

Ninna Braga Moscato

Noelle Kapuy

Norrine Luchsinger

Patricia King

Pyper Davidson

Rachel Wahl

Rhiannon Matthias

Ruby Morris Welling

Sabrina Grosvenor

Samantha Beson

Sarah Lynn Behmlander

Sarah Polglaze

Savanna Bissett

Shawna Kolczynski

Sonaly Rodriguez

Sonia Perez

Stacey Saunders

Stacey Timmons

Stephanie Ditmore

Stephanie Mashia

Stephanie Purpus

Suelee Lee

Tami Garcia

Tamra Whitecotton Mavila

Teri Jackson

Terri Dickey

Tijuana Turner

Tracie Hofacker

Tricia Dransfield

Tricia Marquez-Candelas
Trina Marsh
Valerie Heslep Fisher
Virginia Swanson
Wendy Livingstone

"I can say with great certainty and absolute honesty that I did not know what love was until I knew what love was not." — P.T. Berkey

CHAPTER ONE

LOVE

"A MAN, when he wishes, is the master of his fate." The plaque on the fountain outside my new apartment quotes Andrew Young, and if he were still around today, I'd tell him exactly how wrong he is.

If mastering my fate were as simple as closing my eyes and wishing on stars and throwing pennies into water, I wouldn't be standing here right now.

I throw a quarter toward the trickling water that collects into a mosaic pool of chlorinated water. Wishes have never been my thing, so I let it fall with a gentle plunk. Retrieving a second coin, I flip it in the same direction, only this time it falls short, ricocheting off the granite ledge and rolling down the cement until it disappears beneath a wrought iron bench.

Crawling on my hands and knees, I reach beneath the

empty park bench in search of the runaway quarter, only to come up empty-handed. Literally.

When I was a little girl, long before my father passed away, he'd take me to this fountain just off the main drag of our quaint little town and we'd have coin tossing contests.

He'd assign points: ten for hitting the spitting fish. Twenty if I could slice through a stream. Fifty for whoever could manage to land a coin on the top of the bronzed mermaid's outstretched palm. The loser was supposed to carry the victor home on their shoulders.

Magically, I won every time.

If Dad were still around, he'd hate the hell out of New York City but he'd love the hell out of this fountain outside my apartment. A sculpture of a couple ducking beneath an umbrella centers the display, the man's arm around the woman as water trickles from the top. They're smiling, their marble clothes giving the appearance of being soaked as water splashes up around their feet.

I bet Dad would say it's romantic, much like he was. The man was obsessed with all things love, which was how I got my name—or so the story goes.

Rising, I dust my hands off on my jeans and glance toward the dark windows of my new place just across the cobblestoned, carriage-lighted plaza.

"Here." I thought I was alone, but the velvet tenor of a man's voice proves otherwise. "Take mine."

I wait for my palpitations to settle before turning to face my *generous* benefactor.

Men and their money ...

A disarming smile comes into focus first, under the pale flicker of moonlight and streetlamps, followed by a chiseled jaw with the slightest indentations where dimples should be. His eyes, partially hidden by a pair of tortoiseshell frames, are defined with thick, dark lashes that contrast against his classy machismo.

"No, thank you," I say once I gather my composure. "I was just leaving."

His head tilts and he studies me, and then he turns a shiny quarter between the pads of his fingers.

"You know, your wish won't come true if the coin doesn't hit the water," he says, a hint of a smirk in his tone.

"Is that a fact?" I arch a brow.

"Proven." The handsome stranger nods. "You didn't know that?"

I think he's trying to flirt, but I don't have the energy to tell and even if I did, I wouldn't have the verve to flirt back.

"Fortunately, I don't believe in wishes," I say.

He slides the coin back into his suit pant pocket, followed by his hand, and he stands there, relaxed, like he's got all the time in the world to dedicate to this pointless conversation with a stranger outside a sparkling water fountain. I'm guessing he isn't from the city. Most New Yorkers don't take the time of day to say "excuse me" when they push past you on the sidewalk, let alone offer a replacement quarter to some woman they've never met.

"So you were just ... throwing money into a fountain for ... no reason?" he asks.

"Basically." I sling the strap of my bag over my shoulder, sensing the heavy weight of his stare, and then I turn to leave.

The Jasper on Fifth has been my home for three weeks this Wednesday and it still feels like some unfamiliar vacation rental I'm only inhabiting temporarily. Mom keeps reminding me it won't feel like home overnight and that I need to keep "feathering my nest," but I've already filled it with all the things that no longer remind me of the life I left behind the day I signed those papers, things that help me remember the girl I was before I became the girl I grew up to be. But so far I can't help but feel like an impostor in someone else's clothes, in someone else's home, existing in someone else's world.

I imagine it'll get better with time.

"Hi, Raymond." I greet the nightshift doorman with a small wave as I pass through the lobby.

"Ms. Aldridge." He nods, offering me a smile stained with compassion.

Everyone thinks think they know what happened.

They think they know my story.

They think they know *me*.

They know nothing.

"Good evening, Mr. Warner," Raymond says a second later.

Reaching for the elevator call button, I catch a glimpse of the man who walked in behind me, staring at his expensive shoes and ending with his messy, sandy blond mane and those thick frames that mask the mysterious eyes I met only a moment ago.

The handsome stranger from the fountain stands beside me.

Had no idea he was a neighbor, but then how would I? No one's taken the time to introduce themselves, to welcome me to the building, or to nosily scope out my place under the guise of delivering a tray of Neiman Marcus cookies.

Not that it comes as a surprise.

New York isn't really known for its warm, fuzzy population, and I'm just some woman they read about on Page Six from time to time thanks to my ex.

Clearing my throat, I stare at a set of silver elevator doors emblazoned in monogrammed J's, waiting for the soft chime to tell me this awkward moment will be over soon enough.

One thousand one ...

One thousand two ...

One thousand three ...

One thousand-*ding*.

The doors part and an older woman carrying a white toy poodle under her Chanel-jacketed arm squeezes past us, placing her dog on the tile floor once she's through. The bells on its crystal-studded collar tinkle as it scurries toward the exit.

Raymond pretends to give the dog directions to the nearest restroom. The woman doesn't laugh, but the stranger does.

Stepping inside, I clear my throat, press the button for the seventh floor, and clasp my hands in front of my hips. Staring straight ahead, I avoid eye contact as he takes the spot beside me, unmoving.

"Which floor?" I ask, still staring ahead.

"Seventh. Same as yours."

Interesting. I've been here three weeks and I've yet to see him around because I definitely couldn't forget a face like that.

"Did you just move in?" I ask.

"Few days ago actually."

The elevator deposits us on the seventh floor and the stranger motions for me to step out first. Turns out my generous benefactor is not only my neighbor, but a gentleman to boot.

"Have a nice night," I say, turning down the left hall.

Reaching into my purse, I retrieve my apartment key and head to the last door on the right, only once I get there, I sense a presence behind me. From the corner of my eye, I watch the handsome stranger retrieve his key and slide it into the lock of the door directly across the hall.

"I didn't catch your name," I say. I can't complain about the people in this building being cold and unfriendly and then do the same thing to him after he's been nothing but polite to me.

He turns to face me, capturing my gaze for a moment. "Jude Warner. And you are?"

"Love Aldridge," I say. I'm still not used to going by my maiden name. I've been a LeGrand for almost the entirety of my twenties—the better part of my adult life thus far. But Love LeGrand doesn't exist anymore. I signed her death warrant by way of divorce papers last month, hardly sorry to say goodbye to a poor soul, stuck in the shadows of a disgustingly rich husband who broke every promise he ever made. "Welcome to the building."

With that, I show myself in.

I simply wanted to be cordial, neighborly. Jude seems like a decent man, friendly and approachable, which is rare around these parts, not to mention easy on the eyes ... but meeting new people—men in particular—is the furthest thing from my mind and it's going to be that way for the foreseeable future.

I finally got my heart back from the lying thief who stole it all those years ago, and I'll be damned if I give it away to the first guy who so much as smiles in my direction. I might not be back to my proverbial fighting weight, but I'm not weak by any stretch of the imagination.

Besides, as far as I'm concerned, men are all the same and if one of them wants my heart, he's going to have to pry it out of my cold, dead hands.

Love is for the birds.

Love Aldridge is for herself.

CHAPTER TWO

JUDE

MY NEW PLACE reeks of expensive cologne, fresh flow-ers, and old leather—not that I'm complaining. It's a far cry from the stale pizza-scented two bedroom I've been sharing with my sister and nieces in Brooklyn for the past year. Besides, I've lived in worse places: sweaty Army barracks, tents in Iraq, beer-stained sofas in friends' living rooms.

Sliding my barely-broken in Gucci loafers off, I head to the stainless-steel double-wide fridge and grab a bottle of beer from the middle shelf. There must be twenty different varieties here—most of which I've never heard of. I reach for an Arrogant Bastard, slam the door shut, and twist off the cap.

Standing in the middle of a kitchen bigger than my entire place back in Brooklyn, I drag my palm along the shiny smooth marble counter. Everything's so clean. So untouched. White and marble and wood, chandeliers that look like they belong at the MoMA. Every square inch of this place is doused in upgrades fit for a sheikh, and while this is only my third day here, I still can't help but gawk a little every time I walk through the door.

Earlier today, I'd done a bit of exploring ... mostly drawers and nightstands ... only to find condoms strategically shoved in every corner of this place. I couldn't help but remember that rich bastard's words to me as I left his office that day: "You've got my full permission to drive it like you stole it."

It meaning ... his ex-wife.

But he isn't paying me to judge him, is he?

I take a swig of beer and another good, hard look around.

I've been in places like this plenty of times before, but I was always in a plumber's uniform and I was never there more than a few hours before heading to the next call out.

Making my way to the living room, I stand before a floor-to-ceiling window with an unobstructed view of Central Park.

People pay millions of dollars to live like this and now some rich asshole is paying *me* a million dollars to pretend to live like this for reasons I still don't quite understand. He said he couldn't tell me why for "liability purposes"—his and mine. Maybe that should've been a red flag, and to a guy in different circumstances, that would've been all the reason he needed to walk out of Hunter LeGrand's office right then and there, but as the old adage goes ... he made me an offer I couldn't refuse—literally—because between the lines of that offer was a threat.

Taking a seat in a buttery chair the color of top shelf cognac, I bring the beer bottle to my lips as I take in the view of the city at night. It's a different experience from this side of the bridge, almost like seeing it for the first time.

There are going to be a lot of firsts for me these next few months. First time living like a true Upper Eastsider. First time wearing nothing but designer labels. First time pretending to prefer Chopin and Bach over Bon Iver and Iron and Wine. First time dedicating my entire existence to ensuring some divorcee socialite falls madly, deeply in love with me and then breaking her heart the second the ink is dry on the marriage certificate.

Every time I think about what I'm doing, I hate myself a little bit more than the time before, but if I'm going to do this, I can't think that way. I have to harden my heart, ignore that voice in my head that tells me how fucked up this whole thing is, and keep pushing forward.

Last month, Hunter had given me a small binder full of notes on his ex-wife. Hobbies. Interests. Favorite shops and restaurants. Most-loved travel destinations. Favorite books and movies and wines. Anything I could possibly want to know about her was in there and I was told to study those pages, to know them frontward and backward, to memorize every little thing about Love so that I could morph myself into the kind of man she'd fall irrevocably in love with.

Meeting her tonight for the first time was surreal.

She wasn't at all what I expected, at least not based on the things Hunter had told me. He said Love was materialistic, money-hungry, and stone cold. He said I wouldn't like her at first, that I'd be put off the instant our eyes met. Hunter also described her as spoiled, entitled, and selfish.

But she was wearing faded Levis, throwing money into a fountain just 'cause, and she actually introduced herself and welcomed me to the building.

The only thing that seems to match up so far is the fact

that she's a complete knockout even though the photos Hunter gave me hardly do her justice. In person, Love's got this understated elegance about her, from her soft blonde hair to her hooded hazel eyes, to her pointed nose and high cheekbones. She could be a princess or the girl next door and it would suit her all the same.

And that runner's body... God, I could eat my fist just thinking about it right now. Consummating this relationship will be a piece of fucking cake.

Leaning against the back of my chair, I cross my legs wide and finish my beer, accepting myself for the self-serving piece of shit that I've become, and when I'm done, I force myself to call it a night.

The sooner I go to bed, the sooner I can wake up and get this shit show started.

CHAPTER THREE

LOVE

"THIS REMINDS me of our WVU days," Tierney says as she takes a seat on my bed and scans my new bedroom. "Just hanging out, doing girl stuff."

My best friend smirks, reaching for the newest edition of Elle on my nightstand and aimlessly paging through it.

"Yeah, it does." Seated in a gray velvet chair by the window, I drag my legs in and wrap my arms around them. Tierney sitting on my bed reading one of my magazines does feel like a college flashback, but only until her phone rings and I'm reminded that we're both pushing thirty, she's running her own company while expecting her first baby with her new husband, and we're up to our eyeballs in the "real world."

"I miss those days," she says with a soft sigh. "Life was so damn easy then, wasn't it? I mean, we just woke up, literally rolled out of bed, and did our thing. Biggest concern was where we were going to grab drinks that night."

I miss those days too.

I miss the days when Hunter was nothing but a broke college kid, like myself. I miss the days when he never left my side, when he looked at me with this stupid, goofy grin on his face without even realizing it half the time and my body would fire on all cylinders every time he walked in the room. I miss the five-dollar carnation bouquets and the frozen pizza candlelight dinners. The aimless drives and the dollar-theater movie matinees on free popcorn days.

But money ruins things.

And in the end, it ruined us.

We weren't married but a year when Hunter pitched some cyber security software he'd been coding to some big corporation in Silicon Valley. It was a stretch—him landing a deal on a type of product no one had ever so much as attempted before—but he had my support and nothing to lose, so he went for it.

The day they called with an offer is a day I couldn't forget if I tried. And believe me—I've tried. Many times. It's the day that changed the entire trajectory of our marriage. It's the day the universe took that sweet, beautiful, perfect little thing that we had, doused it in gasoline, and struck an entire book of matches.

I watched us go up in flames, only it wasn't a quick process.

It was a slow burn that played out through harsh words, hurt feelings, through tears and sleepless nights.

Through a text message that was never intended for me ...

To go from having nothing but the clothes on your back,

your young wife, and a shoebox campus town apartment in Morgantown, West Virginia to having tens of millions of dollars dumped in your lap overnight was something Hunter couldn't handle, only neither of us would know it until it was too late.

By the end of that first week, he'd signed a lease on an apartment in some trendy Manhattan neighborhood, sold my vintage Subaru and his used Honda, and rented a moving van—all of this without so much as consulting me.

By the end of the first year, he'd invested in half a dozen startups, the majority of which were profitable and one of which he ended up buying outright: a little company called Blue Stream Records.

And as if we weren't already set for life, the universe decided to make it rain once again a couple of years after Hunter signed a handful of major artists and developed a state-of-the-art streaming service which grew by thousands of users every time we blinked.

The money poured in.

We couldn't stop it.

It was a blessing and then a curse, and it was fun until it wasn't.

"I'm richer than God, Love," Hunter said to me once with a wild look in his dark eyes. And it was always like that. *He* was the rich one. I was just the wife. He was the one with the money and the connections and the overnight notoriety. I was just the girl on his arm who'd loved him before he was anyone special because he was always special to me.

Hunter's business endeavors took us from obscurity to red carpets, from Gap to Givenchy, from a studio apartment to a penthouse.

I'll never forget coming home from a run one day to

someone in my closet, tossing out my entire wardrobe and replacing it with designer pieces she was pulling out of the department store bags that littered the floor.

Hunter had hired her to give me a new look—one that was more appropriate for our new lifestyle. At the time, I thought it was a sweet gesture. It was early in our Manhattan tenure and I thought he was spoiling me, treating me to all the nice things he could never afford before, as a way to celebrate our big move. But now I know it was only a control thing for him.

His insecurities and his bloated ego needed an eleven in a world where everyone in his world were content to have tens.

First it was the wardrobe. Then it was the hair and makeup. The driver. The regular manicures and diamond facials. Then it was the jewelry, the galas, the couture.

But I never wanted any of it.

I only wanted Hunter—the Hunter that I first fell in love with.

We had nothing when we tied the knot, which meant we had no reason to sign a pre-nup, which meant I was entitled to half his earnings as well as alimony.

I didn't want all of that money, but my attorney pushed for it, telling me how much I deserved it for putting up with Hunter all those years, and then he reminded me that I could always give it away.

I found my vindication there, in that suggestion.

That money might have ruined Hunter and obliterated our marriage, but I could still do some good with it.

In the end, despite Hunter retaining one of the best divorce lawyers in the city, I managed to snag a generous lump sum, a handful of assets, and a monthly alimony payment that added up to a whopping eight figures a year.

The *only* way my ex would ever have to stop paying me alimony is if he goes bankrupt or if I remarry—and it'll be a cold day in hell before that happens again.

"Let's go grab a coffee or something," Tierney says, folding the magazine and tossing it aside. "It's either that or I take a nap right here on your brand-new bed."

Smiling, she extends her arms, fingers wiggling with impatience.

Getting up from my chair, I make my way across the room, taking her hands and helping her roll off my bed.

"Need help putting your shoes on too?" I ask.

"Maybe." She winks, and I follow her down the hall toward the little foyer of my apartment. It pales in comparison to the one I had before in the penthouse with Hunter, but I'm perfectly fine with that. In fact, I love that it's cozier. I love how it's comfortable and updated without being pretentious and over the top. The complete opposite of the one I had before. A dainty, flush mount chandelier hangs above us, and I step into my ballet flats while Tierney stuffs her swollen feet into a pair of red-bottomed heels.

I don't tell her she's crazy—she might bite my head off like she did when I asked her if it was okay for her to drink coffee while pregnant. It was an honest question, but she referred me to Google and then gave me her obstetrician's phone number in case I wanted to confirm with her myself.

Screw it.

"We're walking," I remind her. I gave up the driving service when I moved here. Everything I need is within walking distance, and if I want to shed that old LeGrand skin, that means parting ways with unnecessary luxuries like chauffeurs and imported SUVs. "I can loan you a pair of sneakers if you want?"

Tierney looks at me like I'm insane for so much as

suggesting that she's incapable of waddling to the corner in five-inch stilettos whilst seven months pregnant, and then she reaches for the door knob.

Following her to the hall, I pull the door closed and lock up, only when I turn to leave, I see the door across the hall swinging open. A moment later, out steps a shirtless Jude dressed for a summer run in the park—at least I presume. Navy athletic shorts rest low in his angled hips, the inverted muscles of his lower abdomen pointing down before disappearing beneath his waistband. When he rests a hand on his hip, I catch a glimpse of the bulging veins in his arm ... my mind immediately going somewhere else completely.

Our eyes catch and my heart stutters without permission.

Redirecting my thoughts is the easy part. Keeping my body from reacting to a sight like this is the part that'll give me a run for my money.

"Oh. My," Tierney says in a deep Joan Crawford-esque manner, lifting her palm to her chest as she drinks him in. Subtle is a language she's never been able to master.

I mouth the word "sorry" to my neighbor and link my arm into hers in an attempt to drag her away.

"Excuse me," she says to Jude as she jerks her arm from my grasp. "You two are neighbors?"

He looks at me then to her before his full lips pull into a smirk. He's amused.

"We are," he says.

"Have you met yet?" she asks, her finger pointed as it moves between the two of us.

"We have," he says. "Last night."

Turning to me, Tierney's liquid blue eyes widen and she fights a smile. I'm sure the second we're out of here, she's going to go off on me for not mentioning him, but there's nothing to mention.

I have a hot neighbor. So what?

"You know she's single, right?" Tierney says.

"Oh, my god." I turn away for a second. "Tierney. Stop." Glancing back, I say to Jude, "I'm so sorry. She's pregnant and crazy hormonal and she has no filter."

"Are you trying to imply in front of this ridiculously beautiful specimen of a man that I'm a hot mess?" Tierney asks, one auburn eyebrow perched.

"Yep," I say.

"Don't sweat it," Jude says, pulling his phone and earbuds from his shorts pockets. He speaks to her but looks to me. He's still a stranger, but there's something going on behind those olive-green eyes of his that seem to intensify the longer he stares at me. "Love, see you around."

Turning away, Jude heads toward the elevator, but I stay back. It'd be awkward if we all piled in now.

"I can't believe you said that," I say once he's gone, lightly punching her arm before clapping my hand over my mouth. "What are we? Fifteen?"

Tierney laughs. "Lighten up. Your neighbor is hot as hell and you're single as hell. I was just putting that energy out there. If it's meant to be, something will come of it."

"I don't *want* anything to come of anything," I remind her. I've told her this a hundred times this year alone. I don't want to date. I'm focusing on myself for a while and then I'll see what happens. "What if he asks me out now?"

Not that I think he would ...

And for all I know, he's got a wife or fiancée or girlfriend or something.

But still—if he *did* ask me out and I said no, it's going to make bumping into him around The Jasper *real* fun.

"Fine," she says, throwing her hands up as we make our way to the elevator. "I'll leave the divine interventions to fate from now on."

I chuff through my nose.

Good. Because I don't believe in fate.

CHAPTER FOUR

JUDE

"YOU KNOW I still don't agree with any of this," my sister, Lo, sighs into the phone.

"Yep." Pretty sure she made that crystal clear at least thirty-eight times before I left the apartment earlier this week.

"You have my support but not my approval," she says.

She said the same thing when I enlisted in the Army a decade ago.

"Ah. Good to know." As of a few days ago, I had nothing from her but dirty looks and rolled eyes.

"You're a good person, Jude," she says. "And I know you think you're doing this for the right reasons. I know you've justified this a hundred times already. But just ... be careful."

"You guys should come check out the place sometime," I change the subject. What's done is done. The train has left the station. There's no getting off, no turning around. "There's tons of room for the girls to run around. I bet they'd love it."

Lo pauses, and I can just picture her hand smacking across her forehead because she knows I'm redirecting the conversation.

I begin to add that there's a fountain outside they'd love, but I'm interrupted by a knock at the door. Pulling my phone from my ear, I check the time.

10:04 PM.

This is odd.

"Lo, can I call you back?" I ask.

"What's wrong?"

"Someone's at the door. I'll call you back, all right?" I hang up before she has a chance to ask another question, and then I head for the door, squinting through the spyhole and smirking when I see a pretty little blonde standing on the other side of the door.

Taking a closer look, I see she's wrapped in a fluffy white bathrobe.

"Hey," I say, greeting her a moment later. "What's going on?"

She gathers the lapel of her robe in her left hand, the other one holding onto the knot of her belt. "I'm so sorry to bother you. I know it's late. I, uh, I have an issue and I've called the super, and all I got was a voicemail that said it could take twenty-four hours for them to get back to me. I called a plumber, but the quickest anyone could get out here would be two hours from now, and by then my entire apartment might be flooded so—"

"—what happened?"

"I drew myself a bath, walked away for a few minutes, came back and went to shut off the water, only the water won't shut off," she says. "It's like the faucet is broken or something." She worries the left corner of her bottom lip. "I'm so sorry. Maybe you don't even know how to fix something like this, but I just thought I'd ask."

"Yeah. I can take a look for you," I say. Her expression softens and I follow her across the hall, where she leads me through her foyer, past the living room, down a hallway, and across her master bedroom to an all-white bathroom. The standalone tub acts more like a waterfall at this point since the overflow valve can't keep up, and there's a good inch or so of water on her bathroom floor, some of it sopped up with towels.

It takes maybe thirty seconds for me to locate her water shut-off valve and give it a good couple of cranks.

The water stops and Love stands in the doorway with wet feet and a pretty smile on her pink lips.

"How did you know what to do?" she asks.

Rising, I shrug. I can't let her know that I'm a plumber by trade. According to Hunter, I'm a "strategic consultant" with multinational clients. It's exactly the kind of job you can BS because no one really knows exactly what it is you do and contracts are private, so ...

"I might be a little on the handy side," I say.

She smooths her palm over her lapel. "Well, I'm impressed. And grateful. This should buy me some more time until the super can get someone here."

"But you won't have any running water in your bathroom until then," I remind her, hands on my hips as I ponder my next move.

I could fix this issue for her easily. There's usually a missing piece inside the faucet, a screw or part that came loose, but I don't want to give myself away because something like that isn't exactly common handyman knowledge.

But screw it.

She doesn't have time to wait for the super to call her back. By then, her apartment will be so water damaged, she might even have to relocate.

Crouching over the tub, I slip my fingers up the faucet opening and sure enough drag my fingertips across a loose part.

"Got a flashlight?" I ask.

Love turns to leave, returning a few seconds later with a black flashlight, handing it over.

Less than two minutes later, she's back in business.

"Wow ... thank you *so* much," she says, leaning down to grab a soaked towel. "I still don't know how you just *knew* what to do."

Growing up, my father always taught me never to depend on anyone for anything, which was fitting because I couldn't depend on him for shit.

Also didn't hurt that I was a mechanic in the Army. I've never met a valve, part, engine, or apparatus I've never been able to take apart and rebuild.

"What do you do anyway?" she asks. "Like for work? You were dressed so nicely the other night. Wall Street?"

"Nope."

"Banker?"

"Nope," I say.

"What?"

"Strategic consultant." I hope to God I can sell this.

Her brows lift and she nods like she knows what that is. "How'd you get into that?"

"Business major," I lie. I'm so going to hell. "And just ... made the right connections and got the right experience over the years. Wanted to be my own boss. That kind of thing."

"Huh." She studies me, though there's no denying there's an underlying hint that she finds my handy-yet-Upper Eastside persona attractive. I doubt there are many of us.

"What about you? What do you do?" I pivot the conversation.

She snarls her lip for a second then exhales. "Honestly? Nothing."

Love shakes her head, like she's disappointed in herself.

"But I'm meeting with my attorney, going to start up some charitable organizations," she says. "I've recently ... come into some money ... and I plan on giving 95% of it away."

"Only 95%?" I tease.

She laughs a sweet, delicate laugh. "A girl's got to eat."

For a moment, I find myself enjoying this conversation, wet socks and all. There's something unexpectedly down-to-earth about Love, and she's easier to talk to than I anticipated given the fact that we have nothing in common but our current addresses.

"Where are you from?" she asks, slightly squinting.

"I didn't realize you were interviewing me."

She swats my hand. "I'm just asking because you're obviously not from here. You're way too nice."

"You say that like it's a bad thing."

"It's not bad at all. Just ... different. Unexpected," she says. "Yeah. Unexpected. So where are you from?"

Dragging in a long breath, I rub the back of my neck before letting it go. "Everywhere. I'm from everywhere."

Love's nose wrinkles, like she's disappointed in my answer. "Can you be more specific?"

"Moved around a lot. I was a military brat," I say. It's partially true. The year I turned thirteen my father got a dishonorable discharge for beating the ever-loving shit out of my drug-addicted mother and leaving her for dead. After that, he went to prison and we went to live with my aunt in Tulsa before moving in with our grandma in Queens.

"Bet that was interesting."

"Something like that."

Love lifts a brow, giving me a side eye. "I feel like there's more to you than meets the eye. Like you're holding back or something."

"I feel like I came in here to fix your bathtub and now I'm being psychoanalyzed."

She laughs, reaching for a strand of pale hair and tucking it behind her left ear. "Sorry."

I slide my hands in my pockets. "Now it's my turn to ask questions."

Head tilting, she shrugs. "Okay."

"What are you doing Friday night?"

Silence.

Dead silence.

Her honey-hazel eyes flick to the wet floor as her lips part and then seal shut again.

"This is about what Tierney said earlier..." she says, finally glancing up at me as her voice trails off. "Seriously, you don't have to do this."

"This has nothing to do with what your friend said." I pull my shoulders back and flash a confident smirk, laser focused on my target. "I want to take you out."

I swear she blushes for a moment, but it vanishes just as quickly as it appeared. There's a bit of modesty under that poised façade.

"Seven o'clock?" I ask.

"Jude." The way she says my name tells me the answer

to my question. "I'm so sorry. You seem like a really nice guy, but I'm not dating right now."

Shot down.

I offer a gracious smile and make my way across her bathroom with sopping wet socks. Talk about kicking a man when he's down.

Not that this date would've been real, but I didn't think being turned down would bruise my ego this much.

Love walks me to the door, keeping a few paces behind, and I show myself out to the hallway.

"I've just gone through a divorce and I'm sort of putting the pieces of my life back together. Dating isn't really on my radar right now," she says again, lifting her pink nails to her pink mouth. Everything about her is velvet and delicate and I wonder how the hell she survives in a city that eats nails for breakfast. "Truly, I'm so sorry."

"Don't be," I say. "I get it."

She smiles, resting her cheek against the open door. "Thank you."

"For what?" I ask.

"For being such a gentleman," she says, her voice pillow soft. "You're a class act, Jude Warner."

If she only knew.

CHAPTER FIVE

LOVE

GROWING UP, I never aspired to be a kept woman. I never wanted to live in a high-rise luxury apartment in one of the most expensive cities in the world. I never wanted to be that woman who kept herself busy between nine AM and five PM and then pounced on her husband the second he came home from work like some sex-starved centerfold.

I wanted a simple life.

A loving marriage. A happy home. A fulfilling career. A baby or two when the time was right.

"Sign here, Love," Richard Wexler, my attorney, slides a stack of papers across his desk and points to the little sticky neon arrow at the bottom. "And on the next page."

He's helping me set up my first charity, Agenda W, which is aimed at helping women get back on their feet after life-changing events. We'll provide job training, scholarships, resources ... all the tools they might need to ensure they can make it on their own without the help of a man.

My real estate agent is going to help me find a space for it in Brooklyn where we can get more space for less money, and I'm going to spend the next six months or so getting it up and running.

This ... this is step one.

Richard slides another stack of paperwork toward me. "This is establishing that you're a not-for-profit organization."

I sign my name at the bottom of the page.

"You're a very kind person," Richard says in his born-and-bred New York accent. "I know you're going to do good things in this world."

"Thank you, Richard," I say, capping the pen and placing it diagonally across the signed stack. "That's my plan."

Freedom—especially financial—is still a foreign concept to me. Even as a married woman, I never had my own money. My bank account was always shared with Hunter and the daily limit was so small sometimes I had to split my purchases between my debit card and the spare AmEx he gave me for emergency purposes.

A few times over the years, I'd try to discuss the money situation with him, but it would never end well. He would quickly become agitated, shoot down my suggestions, disqualify all of my reasons for needing my own account. Once I told him I was looking for a job and he wasted no time reminding me that our travel schedule wasn't conducive to me working outside the home ... and he was right. I accompanied Hunter to every event, be it local, nationwide, or global. We were gone just as much as we were home.

He had me exactly where he wanted me.

Despite the fact that he claimed to be "richer than God," Hunter was still a tightwad—but only when it came to everyone but himself.

One Christmas, he gave me a Gucci bag. The strap broke after a couple of months, so I took it into the Gucci store in SoHo where the clerk proceeded to inform me that it was, indeed, a fake.

"A very *good* fake," she said.

But a fake nonetheless.

Cheap bastard.

Growing up underprivileged, I think Hunter always had this deep-seated fear of losing it all, so he clung to it so tightly, so selfishly, that in the end he did lose it all. He lost the only person who ever truly loved him when he had nothing to give but a kiss and a smile and the heart beating in his chest.

Only I don't know if he'll ever realize that.

"I'll get this filed today," Richard says, standing up and smoothing his red satin tie down his shirt.

A moment later, he walks me to the lobby, and I ride the elevator to the main level, only it stops at the fourth floor first, picking up a man with dark hair and the same tortoise-shell frames Jude was wearing the night I met him.

I still can't believe he asked me out last night, and I'm absolutely blaming Tierney, even if he says her little comment had nothing to do with it.

But I suppose there's nothing wrong with hanging out sometime ...

I could see myself being friends with him, though it might be a bit of a challenge to keep my eyes where they belong. The other night when he was fixing my faucet, I caught myself staring so hard at him that I forgot to breathe, studying the way his broad shoulders strained against his shirt, the way he raked his hands against his strong jaw, how his dark lashes framed his striking, almond-shaped gaze.

Just hope he didn't notice.

Heading back to The Jasper, I mull over my next steps for Agenda W. Jude mentioned he was some kind of strategic consultant. I wonder if he could help me or at least point me in the right direction? Maybe charities and NFP organizations aren't in his wheelhouse, but it doesn't hurt to ask, and if he can't help, maybe he'll know someone who can?

Thirty minutes later, I'm making my way down our shared hallway.

I don't know his schedule, I don't know when he works from home or when he travels, and I hate to just pop over unexpected again, but not having his number leaves me with no other choice.

Clearing my throat, I square my shoulders with his door and give it a knock. From where I stand, I can almost make out voices. Plural. And the pounding of footsteps, like someone's running.

Shit.

He must have company.

A moment later, the door swings open and a young woman not much younger than me stands at the threshold with a toddler on her hip. With straight dark hair cut into a bob, bangs straight across her forehead, tight jeans, a white cotton tank top, and ruby red lips, she's as bold as she is eye-catching.

"Hi," I say. "I was just looking for Jude."

She says nothing, taking me in from head to toe, though not in a way that makes me feel uncomfortable. It's quite possible that I look familiar to her. For the better part of last year, my picture was prominently featured in Us Weekly, Star Magazine, OK!, and even People.com. I get these kind of looks everywhere I go, at least once a day. People squint and stare and search my face as they try to place me in their mind's eye.

"I live across the hall," I add, breaking the silence.

The toddler stares at me, unblinking, and another little girl squeezes between the raven-haired beauty and the doorjamb.

"Who is this, Mommy?" the older girl asks.

Before she has a chance to answer, the door widens a little more and Jude appears. Scratching his temple, he offers a half-smile that almost makes me forget what I came here for, but seeing the four of them standing together, so comfortably close, so natural and united, makes me realize this might be his ex or baby mama or whatever and these girls might be his daughters.

And that's perfectly fine—it's not like it changes anything.

"I didn't know you were busy," I say, taking a step toward my door. "I can come by another time."

"No, no, it's fine," he says before turning to the woman. "I'll be back in a sec."

Slipping out into the hallway, he pulls the door closed behind him and aligns himself with me. The faint scent of his spicy cologne fills my lungs, though there's something familiar about it, like it's something Hunter would've worn ... which is slightly disappointing, but I won't let it ruin my impression of him just yet.

"That's my sister, Lo," he says. I wasn't going to ask because it's none of my business and I didn't want to pry. "And my nieces, Piper and Ellie. They were just coming by to check out the new place."

"Are they from around here?"

"Brooklyn." His eyes haven't left mine once. "So what's going on?"

I wave my hand. "I had something to ask you, but we can talk later. I don't want to hold you up."

He arches a brow. "So you're just going to leave me hanging?"

"It's nothing. Really. It can wait," I say.

Jude checks his watch. "Was going to take my sister and nieces out for a late lunch, but now I'm going to be distracted the entire time."

"Fine," I say, pretending to wave an imaginary white flag. "I was just going to ask if you'd be interested in consulting for me."

His hand lifts to his jaw, partially covering his full mouth as his brows meet, and then he stares over my shoulder, lost in thought.

"You can think about it," I say, sensing his hesitation. "I don't even know what your schedule is like. Maybe you're booked out. I don't know."

Stop rambling, Love...

Jude exhales and I brace myself for a "no," which is fine. I came here with zero expectations.

"Why don't we talk about this over dinner?" he asks. "Friday night. Seven o'clock."

The tension between us is thick, ripe. Ready to be plucked and devoured.

"Oh, you're smooth, Jude Warner," I say, head tilted and finger pointed as I step backwards toward my door.

He wears the smile of an Olympic gold medalist, his hands resting in his pockets as he shrugs his shoulders.

"So that's a yes?" he asks.

"It's not a date," I say.

"Okay."

"It's a *work* dinner," I add.

"Sure." He reaches for his door knob, eyes lit. "See you Friday."

He disappears into his apartment, and I turn toward mine, whispering *"work dinner"* under my breath a half a dozen times as I head inside with sweaty palms and a swirl of butterflies in my middle, the very things I haven't felt since I was eighteen, the things I promised myself not to feel again until I'm ready.

I lock the door behind me and press my back against it, composing my liquefied self as the space around me spins like a carousel. My head is light—the way it gets after a few too many glasses of champagne.

I'm pretty sure this is what excitement feels like, something I haven't felt in years.

Drawing in a long, cool breath, I let it go and stride down the hall toward my bedroom to peel out of these clothes and slip into some pajamas so I can order takeout and binge watch the rest of *The Crown*.

I need a distraction. I need to focus on something else.

Clearly my head and my body are on two entirely different pages when it comes to my impending dinner with the guy across the hall.

Here's hoping my heart stays the hell out of this.

CHAPTER SIX

JUDE

"YOU KNOW she's way too good for you, right?" Lo says, rocking Ellie on her hip as she stands in my kitchen.

"Yep."

"Like ... *way*." She laughs through her nose, studying my outfit. "It's weird seeing you like this."

"Like what?"

Lo rolls her eyes. "You know. No ripped jeans or vintage Ramones t-shirts. Hair actually combed for once."

I know I look like a schmuck with my pressed slacks and cashmere sweater and shiny Italian loafers and hair parted on the side and slicked with brill cream, but this is all part of Hunter's master plan.

"If you want to hook Love, you have to use the right bait," he'd said, comparing his ex-wife to a fucking fish.

"God, this place is amazing," Lo says, carrying Ellie

from the kitchen to the living room, where she hones in on the kind of view we only ever dreamed of.

"Sure beats our fourth floor walk-up."

She smirks. "Yeah. Just a little."

"I Venmo'd you the rent money this morning," I said. "Next six months are covered. There's some extra for food and Piper's meds."

Lo turns to me, her smart-ass expression fading. She's tough as rocks, but I swear I see a hint of tears brimming in her eyes. She doesn't have to say a word. I know what this means to her. After her deadbeat ex was hauled off to prison a couple years back for running drugs (unbeknownst to all of us), she found herself a twenty-three-year-old single mother with a toddler and a newborn, no job, and no way to feed them.

At the time, I'd been out of the Army for a few years, had just finished my plumbing apprenticeship, and landed a decent job at Premier Plumb and Supply in Brooklyn. As soon as Lo finally admitted to me that she was struggling and about to become evicted, I found a hole-in-the-wall two-bedroom above a pizza shop and moved them in, vowing to help her get on her feet.

Now, during the day, Lo stays home with the girls. At night she waits tables at some exclusive restaurant on 67th Street, heading into the city shortly after the girls go down for the night. Tips are decent and the hours are shit, but she doesn't complain because this has always been temporary.

The plan was for her to start nursing school at Touro, and she was going to start this summer. But I lost my job a few months back due to cutbacks, and one of us had to make sure the rent was still being paid.

"You sure you want to do this?" Lo asks, biting her lower lip as Ellie runs her chubby fingers through her hair.

Piper is seated in the cognac chair across from the TV, messing with a remote that I'm pretty sure belongs to the fireplace.

"What choice do I have?" I'd spent the last three months applying for jobs, but all the ones I could find had shitty pay, zero benefits, or shady reputations. I booked every music gig I could find, playing at any bar that would so much as take me for an hour or two at night, but it didn't make up for the lost wages, and most of it went toward Piper's meds anyway.

"We could always move," she says.

"It costs money to move, Lo. And we don't have that right now." My tone is short and I don't mean to come at her that way, but I don't need to be reminded that what I'm doing is nothing less than heartless. "As soon as this is over, we can look into moving somewhere cheap and safe. With good people and even better schools. All this stress, this bullshit? It's about to end."

Taking a seat at a kitchen bar stool, I slump my elbow on the counter and exhale.

"She seems really nice," Lo says. "Sweet."

"I know."

"And she just went through a divorce," she adds. "She's probably already heartbroken. And you're just going to come in and—"

Fuck. "*I know.*"

Lo doesn't manage our finances. She doesn't see that we're one rough month away from being out on the street, one unexpected bill away from Piper not having her EpiPen or inhaler when she needs it.

A million dollars and a record deal.

That's what this deal is worth to Hunter LeGrand, that's what he laid on the table. And before I had a chance to so much as think it over, he was elaborating on the fact that he's "well connected" and he can "make shit happen" and he has no qualms about "blacklisting people like you" should they deserve it. He also felt the need to remind me that singer-songwriters like me were on every street corner in Manhattan, that I could always make a living busking in the subways or singing covers on YouTube if this deal didn't pan out because he'd personally see to it that my name would *never* be in lights.

"The girls are probably hungry," I say to Lo, checking my watch. "Let's grab something."

My sister moves Ellie to her other hip, her eyes snapping to the floor. "It's okay. We should get going so we can catch the five."

"I thought I was taking you guys out for lunch ... made us reservations at Serendipity III."

"I'm sorry, Jude. After seeing her ... it just doesn't feel right spending your blood money on frozen hot chocolate."

My sister can be so fucking dramatic sometimes.

"It's not blood money, Lo," I say, half-chuckling. "No one's getting offed."

"You know what I mean." She speaks quickly and her gaze moves to mine. "Come on, Pipes. Let's go."

Piper places the fireplace remote on the table where she found it and slides off the leather chair, dashing across the living room toward her mother, her dark pigtails bouncing.

A second later, the three of them head to the door, only before they leave, Lo turns to me. "The place is great and all, Jude, but don't get too comfortable in case this whole thing blows up in your face. Because it will. And when it does, don't say I didn't warn you."

They leave before I have a chance to respond, and I'm left with my kid sister's words echoing in my head, resonating off the deepest fragments of my conscience and all the parts of me that wish I never walked into Blue Stream Records that random Tuesday in May, flash drive demo in hand, and crossed paths with the CEO himself in the elevator lobby.

I should've known when Hunter said, "I don't normally take unsolicited demos, but you seem like exactly the kind of act I'm looking for right now," that he wasn't talking about music.

Not at all.

CHAPTER SEVEN

LOVE

"WHAT ARE YOU WEARING RIGHT NOW?"

I smirk at my reflection in the mirror as Tierney's voice comes through the speakerphone.

"Something appropriate for a business dinner," I say, fastening a modest diamond stud into my right ear before attending to the next.

She exhales into the phone. "Bo-ring."

"That's all this is. We're discussing how to get Agenda W off the ground. Nothing more, nothing less." I dig through my makeup bag in search of my blush and bronzer compact.

"You're killing me, Love," Tierney says. "I'm not saying you need to rush back out there and find a man, but there's nothing wrong with having fun. Casual dating does not equal marriage."

The last time I casually dated anyone was in college,

when I met Hunter LeGrand in Econ 101 and he asked me to study with him over pizza one night. We were inseparable after that, and there was never anyone else after him, so my dating history is akin to a blank piece of paper at this point.

"Right. I know that," I say, tapping my blush brush in a compact of Nars Orgasm before sweeping it across the apples of my cheeks. "And that'd be fine if this is what that was, but like I said, this is a work thing."

Tierney laughs. "Whatever you want to call it is fine, but I guaran-freaking-tee you he's going to try to kiss you at some point tonight."

"Let him try." I laugh, clasping the compact shut before reaching for my mascara, ironically called Better Than Sex.

I sense a theme here but it's pure coincidence, I swear.

"He's going to be here any minute," I say, checking the time on my phone screen.

"Call me tomorrow," she says. "Tell me everything."

Rolling my eyes, I give her my word before pressing the red button.

Finishing my lashes, I toss everything back in my makeup drawer and head to my closet to step into my Valentino flats in basic black. Heels scream "fuck me," especially on a Friday night, so I figured flats would send the right message. Plus, they complement my black pencil skirt and white button-down blouse. My hair is down, pressed sleek and straight and parted deep on one side, finishing off my look.

I need to look serious, like a woman trying to launch a business operation, not like I'm looking to get a piece.

Tucking a strand of hair behind my left ear, I give myself a final once-over in the mirror just as the knock at my door echoes down the hallway.

He's here.

Smoothing my hands down the front of my dress, I take my time heading to the door, grabbing my clutch off the console in the foyer and softly clearing my throat before answering.

"Hey." Jude stands at my threshold, his hands resting in the pockets of slim-cut khakis that show off his runner's legs. A crisp, fitted white button down hugs his upper body, straining against his tight chest and broad shoulders. A belt with a silver "H" buckle—Hermes—ties the look together. For a second, I almost see Hunter standing before me as this is exactly the kind of outfit he'd have worn for a casual dinner, but I force his image out of my mind. "We match."

He points to his shirt and then mine as he winks, which somehow immediately puts me at ease when I didn't even realize I wasn't at ease in the first place. My breathing slows and steadies and I laugh at his cheesy attempt at making a joke.

"Seriously though, you look nice," he says, eyes dragging the length of me, his intense gaze lingering in certain areas for a beat longer than necessary.

"You aren't supposed to say things like that when it's a business dinner," I remind him, stepping out of my apartment and locking the door behind me.

"Thanks for the reminder. It must have slipped my mind." Jude places his hand on the small of my back, sending an unanticipated quiver down my spine, and then he guides me toward his apartment door.

"Did you forget something?"

"Nope." He reaches for the knob and a second later the door swings open.

His place is dark, save for the flicker of candles set at his dining room table and the sparkle of the city lights filtering in through his living room window.

"Jude ..."

Two silver cloches rest at two silver place settings at the table, and a chilled bottle of wine nestled in a bucket of ice sits beside the candlelit centerpiece.

"I ordered in," he says. "Hope that's okay. I find restaurants can be too distracting, especially on Friday nights. It's just not conducive to a business meeting."

"Were candles and wine really necessary?" I'm standing in his doorway now.

"The catering company did all of that," he says with a shrug. I think I believe him. Hunter used to hire a caterer sometimes for our hosted dinner parties, and they'd do the same thing with the candles and the wine. "Would've been the same way at the restaurant."

True.

"Anyway, I hope you don't mind. I got you the petit filet with the gunpowder crust," he says. "Side of scallops."

I always used to order that exact meal from Maestros.

"How'd you know I like those things?" I ask. I still haven't taken a single step.

"I didn't." He makes his way to his dining room table, lifting the cloche from his plate. "Figured everyone likes either seafood or steak, so I got you both just to be safe." Jude's green gaze lifts toward mine. "You're not a vegetarian, right?"

I shake my head and his mouth curls at the side. He's so casual, so natural around me, and I can't help but feel like I've known him longer than I have.

"You going to come in and eat?" he asks. "Or you just going to stand there like I'm Hannibal Lecter about to serve you braised brain and Chianti?"

"Sorry," I say, finally closing the door behind me. "I guess this just wasn't what I was expecting. A little taken aback."

"If you want, we can ditch this entire thing and go grab a slice of pizza?" he offers. "I'm just as comfortable talking business under fluorescent lights."

There's something fascinating about Jude, something contradictory in the way he looks so high brow but speaks to me like the boy next door. He wears Gucci shoes but cracks lame jokes and doesn't take anything seriously. He smiles at me constantly, and it isn't a creepy smile, but one that makes my heart do the tiniest somersaults sometimes.

The way he acts completely challenges the way he looks, and I've never met anyone like him. Didn't even know guys like him existed, least of all in the Upper East Side.

"No, this is fine." I take a seat across from him, lifting my cloche and placing it aside. The familiar peppery scent of the seasoned steak fills my lungs and for a moment, I glance across the candlelit table and see Hunter seated across from me. My stomach knots until Jude's face comes into focus. I'd take him up on that pizza offer, but he already put so much thought and planning into this dinner.

"All right, so tell me about your business," he says, rising over the table to pour our wines.

Sitting straight, I say, "It's a not-for-profit organization called Agenda W. We're aimed at helping women get on their feet and find financial independence."

His lips press together and he nods. "All right. I like that. Continue."

"We'll offer scholarships, resources and referrals, child-care for women attending job interviews," I say. "We'll have a clothes closet for women needing professional wardrobes as they look for jobs. Basically, in my mind, it's a one-stop shop where we can help women rise up, find freedom in their independence, and take care of themselves and their families without relying on anyone or anything else." I pull in a deep breath as the candlelight flickers against his face, lighting a glint in his green eyes. "I know places like this exist all over the city and I know I'm not bringing anything new to the table, but I don't think it's possible to have too many of these. One more is one more, and that's a good thing."

"Agree," he says, brows meeting. "And how are you funding this? Donations?"

"It'll be fully self-funded," I say, not wanting to get into specifics. I've already spoken with my accountant, who confirmed that the interest from the first year of my alimony alone would more than cover start-up costs and should sustain us for the foreseeable future.

He doesn't act surprised, doesn't show a hint of disbelief. "And what about staffing?"

"We'll start with the basics," I say. "A front desk person, a counselor, a social worker, an education advisor, a child-care provider. We'll add as we grow."

Jude slices into his steak. "It sounds like you have it all figured out."

"I know," I say, "but I keep feeling like I'm missing something. Kind of just winging this thing."

"You'll need liability insurance, payroll," he says, pointing his fork. "And a marketing plan. Some PR, too. But this isn't really what I do, Love. Typically, I guide companies toward decisions that help place them above their competition and optimize their profitability. You're not-for-profit. Competition isn't a thing for you. Your biggest hurdle will be spreading the word and making sure everyone knows who Agenda W is and what they do."

He speaks with confidence, shedding his boy-next-door-ness and switching into the skin of a businessman with the unstoppable ability to make difficult decisions and get results.

I'd be lying to myself if I ignored how sexy that is.

"I really appreciate this," I tell him, forking a tender scallop. "I know this isn't your area of expertise, but just knowing I have someone to talk to about this takes a little bit of the pressure off. I mean, I have Tierney and she runs her own business, but she inherited it from her aunt. She knows nothing about starting from scratch, you know?"

He nods, reaching for his wine glass. "I'm happy to help anyway I can, Love."

Jude smiles before taking a sip, and I relish the way he says my name, so soft, so natural, like it belongs right there on his tongue and on that full mouth of his.

He's disarming me like a bomb technician dismantles an explosive, with the kind of skill and patience that make it seem natural and easy.

I need a deep breath.

I need to look away.

I need to harden my resolve and stay strong and not get swept up in this man's charms.

"Anyway," I say, "I've got a meeting with a graphic designer next week to go over logo mockups ..."

I take the wheel of the conversation, ensuring we're headed in the right direction, not stopping for any non-business-related detours, and by the time we finished dinner, I've managed to bring us safely to our final destination.

I'm not sure what time it is, but the city view from his window is aglow with a full moon, cherry-colored traffic tail-lights, and Central Park street lamps. Rising, I take my wine glass and head toward the picturesque view, the same one I have from my bedroom as our apartments must intersect, wrapping around this corner of the building.

"We share this view, you know," I say, only he wouldn't know. He's only been in my place once, and I had my bedroom curtains drawn. "Isn't it incredible?"

Hunter always wanted to live in the trendier neighborhoods with the younger crowd. Once when I brought up living uptown, he scoffed at me and told me I had terrible taste in locations. So of course, as soon as the divorce papers were served, I called up my real estate agent and had her find me the perfect place with a view of Central Park.

"It is," he says, taking the spot next to me. "A million-dollar view reserved only for the fortunate few."

The tiniest hint of resentment lies in his tone, and he shakes his head as he stares out the window.

"We're lucky," I say. "That's for sure. We didn't have views like this back in West Virginia."

I wait for him to ask me something personal, but a question never comes. And actually, this entire night he's yet to divert a single conversation into a "getting to know you" session. It's like he's actually respecting my "this is not a date" stance.

Exhaling, I fight a smirk before hiding it in my wine glass. I don't even think I could find something to dislike about him if I tried. He's polite, professional, and charming, and I'm one hundred percent at ease with him.

But I can't help thinking about that old cliché my mother used to say all the time. "If it seems too good to be true, it probably is."

Jude is absolutely too good to be true.

And maybe *that's* the thing I should dislike about him?

No one is this perfect, this flawless. No one's this kind

and this genuine and this easy to be around *and* ridiculously attractive on top of it all.

Feeling the heaviness of his stare, I turn and glance up at him.

"What?" I ask, not knowing how long he'd been watching me. It's been a long time since anyone looked at me like that—studying me like I'm some fascinating creature, drinking me in like I'm a sight to see. "What are you thinking about right now?"

He smirks. "Nothing."

Rolling my eyes, I bump my elbow into his arm. "Right. So you're staring at me and thinking absolutely nothing."

"People can do that, you know," he says. "Just like they can throw coins in a fountain for no reason at all."

"Touché. Seriously though, I can't leave here tonight without an answer," I tease, knowing full well it doesn't matter what he was thinking, but my curiosity is going to keep me awake at night if I don't find out.

"You're leaving?" he asks, head jutting back as if I've just shocked him.

"Our business dinner's over."

"Yeah, but I still have half a bottle of very nice wine over there. If you leave, I'm going to have to finish it myself and that's kind of sad, don't you think?"

I raise my left hand. "I'm not one to judge, so no. I don't think that's sad. You bought the wine and you should enjoy the hell out of it guilt free."

Jude inhales, lifting his hand to the back of his neck as he pivots to glance out the window. There's almost this nervous energy about him, one that wasn't there before, like he can't stand still, and I get the impression there's something more he wants to say.

"I should go," I say, placing my hand on his shoulder.

"Thank you so much for tonight. I'll keep you posted on everything. And feel free to send me a bill for your time."

His brows furrow. I think I've insulted him, but I don't want him to think I'm entitled or that I'm assuming his advice came free of charge after he arranged for this incredible dinner.

"Love ..." he says my name as his eyes fall to my mouth for a short second, but long enough for me to notice.

The sails are shifting, the wind blowing us in a different direction, and this is where I jump ship.

"Goodnight, Jude," I say, placing my empty stemware on his counter before grabbing my clutch. "Thanks again for your help."

With that, I duck out of there before he has a chance to try to kiss me.

And before I have a chance to let him.

CHAPTER EIGHT

JUDE

I CHANGE out of my *bougie* clothes, pour the hundred-dollar bottle of wine down the sink in the butler's pantry, and cap off the night with a cold beer and some sports highlights.

Tonight was intense at times, but I think I managed to pull it off. I had no fucking clue what a "strategic business consultant" even did, but an hour before I went to get her, I did enough internet research that I got the gist of it.

She seemed to buy it.

That said, while I wasn't busy being a deceptive bastard, I actually enjoyed my evening with her. The food was perfection and the view was amazing (and I'm not just talking about the cityscape outside my window). There were times I almost forgot that this wasn't real, times I caught myself wondering what it might be like to taste those rosebud lips and bury my fingers in that soft, sunshine-blonde hair.

Taking a swig of beer, I place it on a coaster and massage my temple.

I almost kissed her tonight. At first, I was on the fence, wondering if the timing would seem random, but we were standing there, the mood was set, her voice was soft, and her eyes were sparkling. It was all but a written invitation to make a move, but as soon as she so much as picked up on what I was about to do, she bolted.

I'm not sure how the hell I'm going to take us from this to walking down the aisle in a little under six months or why the hell Hunter thought that was even a possibility. He made it sound like this was going to be a cakewalk, that she was lonesome and eager and she'd practically jump into my arms like a rescue dog begging for someone to love them.

It's almost like he set me up to fail by placing an impossible task in my hands.

Or maybe he doesn't know his former wife as well as he thought. Maybe he had her all wrong? There's also a chance the divorce changed her in a way that Hunter never anticipated or isn't aware of.

Either way, I like a challenge, but I may have bitten off more than I can chew with this arrangement. Threats and dollar signs will do that to a broke and desperate man.

Finishing my beer, I carry it to the sink and give it a rinse before tossing it in the recycling bin. Everything here is so proper, so organized, completely opposite of my place in Brooklyn where you can't go more than two steps without stepping over Cabbage Patch babies and toddler-friendly Lego pieces, where the trash is always overflowing and we don't even own a recycling bin because there's no room for one in our microscopic kitchenette.

But still, there's a part of me that won't let myself enjoy this.

I don't deserve to.

Making my way down the hall, I stop when I hear the soft pats of a late night knock at my door. Turning back, I head for the door, glancing out the spyhole. The corners of my mouth curl up when I see Love standing there.

She came back ...

I smirk.

"This is unexpected," I say when I greet her a second later.

Love's eyes lock onto mine and her tongue traces her lower lip before she begins to say something, but I don't give her a chance to speak before pulling her in and closing the door. I'm being forward as hell and I know it, but I've got to seize this moment before it's gone for good because God only knows when I'm going to have another opportunity to make a move.

"Jude ..." my name is a breath on her lips, the very ones I'm about to claim.

Sliding my hand along the side of her soft jaw, I lower my mouth to hers, bracing her against the door as her body melts against mine. She exhales, the scent of wine filling the space around us, and I taste tonight's wine on her pillowed lips before our tongues collide.

I knew it.

I knew she wanted this.

Confident in my choice, I kiss her harder, my fingers buried in her soft hair and free hand curling behind her hip, pressing her body tight against mine.

"Jude ..." she says my name once more, coming up for air. Her mouth is pink, her chest rising and falling in quick little spurts, and her eyes search mine. "I ... I forgot my phone."

Fuck. Me.

Backing away and feeling like a jackass, I lift my hands into a wordless apology.

Heading toward the table in my entry, she locates her phone, lifting it to show me as she offers a gracious smile. "It must have fallen out of my bag."

"I, uh ... wow. Um. I'm so sorry, Love," I say, massaging the back of my neck, head tucked. "Guess I was excited to see you and got a little ahead of myself."

Rubbing her lips together, she winks. "I'll let it slide ... but just this once."

Turning, she shows herself out.

And I stand here alone, reveling in the fact that she kissed me back.

Love kissed me back.

And if that isn't a sign of what's to come, I don't know what is.

CHAPTER NINE

LOVE

NO ONE HAS *EVER* KISSED me like that.

Not Jared Kepner in the seventh grade.

Not my high school boyfriend, Robbie Smart.

Not my ex or anyone in between.

Pacing my apartment with Jude's taste on my tongue, I try my damnedest to ignore the 100 mile-per-hour beat of my heart and the electric charges igniting every nerve ending in my body.

It was just a kiss.

I'm a single woman.

I'm a free woman.

I'm allowed to have fun.

This doesn't mean we're dating.

And *most importantly*, this doesn't mean we're *going to* date.

Even if I was in a place where I was ready to get back

out there, Jude is exactly the kind of guy I *don't* need. In all his glorious perfection, he's got heartbreak written all over. I see it on that chiseled, flawless face of his and etched in those dusty green irises I lose myself in when I'm not being careful.

Plus, there's something about him that reminds me of my ex. The clothes? The cologne? The confidence? At least their personalities are different. Jude charms and disarms. Hunter never had that innate charisma, only the ability to fake it.

With wine-flooded veins and my body still reeling from that toe-curling, electrifying kiss, I close my eyes, lift my fingers to my lips, and trace the warmth that still lingers as I accept one simple, inarguable truth: there's nothing wrong with kissing insanely hot men for the thrill of it.

And who knows? I might even do it again sometime.

CHAPTER TEN

JUDE

THE ELEVATOR DOORS part the next morning, and I take a step forward just as Love takes a step out.

"Oh, hey," she says, almost brushing against me.

I let the elevator go. I'll catch the next one.

"Hey." I smile and act natural despite the fact that she seems to be having a hard time maintaining eye contact with me. We kissed for a hot minute last night. There's no need for this to be awkward.

"Heading out?" she asks. There's a rosy flush to her cheeks and her sunny hair is piled high on top of her head. A thin gray sweatshirt with a gaping neck hangs over her willowy shoulders, revealing the black and neon yellow straps of a sports bra and workout top beneath.

"Dry cleaner's." I nod toward the hangered clothes I've flung over my back. Can't remember the last time I owned any clothes that required professional cleaning, but this is apparently who I am now. "You?"

"Just got back from spin class," she says. "Hey, I'm going to Brooklyn in a couple hours to check out this space I'm thinking of leasing for Agenda W."

"Brooklyn?" I ask.

She nods.

"You need a second opinion on the location? I'm pretty familiar. Spend a lot of time there with Lo and the girls."

Her teeth rake across her bottom lip as her brows knit. "Really? You don't have to do that. I'm sure you've got better things to do."

"Nah, I don't mind."

Love's head tilts to the side. "I'd feel bad. Seriously. My Realtor will be there and—"

"Love," I say, cutting her off. "It's never a bad thing to get a second opinion, and that's my *professional* opinion." Checking my watch, I pause for a moment. I don't want to seem like I'm constantly available and I don't want to jump at every opportunity to be with her—which I'm epically failing at thus far. Coming on too strong, too fast could be too much, and once you cross that line, there's no going back. "I've got a conference call in an hour, but I can move a few things around this afternoon."

I sound like such a fucking douche.

And then I remember: I *am* a fucking douche.

Love offers a gentle smile, her gaze softening and her shoulders relaxing. "You sure?"

Nodding, I smile back. "Of course."

"Perfect. Meet you back here around two?"

———

"THIS IS IT." Love hooks her hand into my elbow and pulls me to the middle of an old bread factory-turned-office space just off Neptune Avenue.

The space is wide open, brick walls and brand new black-trimmed windows with the Pella stickers still on. The floors are concrete and the space has a modern coffee-shop vibe going on.

"I was expecting more of a community center type of feel or like a church basement vibe," I say, "but this is nice."

"See, that's where I'm taking things in a different direction. When women come to Agenda W, I want them to want to be here, to not feel like a charity case. Some of those places are so depressing, you know? And I want people to leave here feeling good about themselves because that's ultimately what's going to determine what happens after that."

Love talks with her hands, her golden eyes lit from within as she paces the expansive layout. The soles of her ballet shoes tap and echo and her real estate agent stands back, quietly composing an email on her phone while we take a look around.

"Over here," she says. "There are eight office suites, a conference room which we'll probably use for childcare, a fully renovated restroom, and a breakroom with a kitchenette." Love takes a few steps before turning back to me. "You said your sister lives in Brooklyn, right?"

"She does. My nieces too."

"So you're pretty familiar with the area."

"Very."

"So what are your thoughts on the location, then?" she asks, glancing toward the windows where pockets of people amble down the sidewalk.

"It's perfect, actually," I say. "There's a YWCA down the street, which would be good for referrals and partnerships. And you've got public transit stops right outside here so there's your easy access. There's a really good deli on the corner. Line's out the door during the lunch hour so there's some good PR. People will see your sign and start talking. Everyone loves when something new comes around. I can ask Lo what she thinks about the location too, but I'm pretty sure she'll agree."

"How do you know that much about Brooklyn if you only come here to visit family?" She squints, head slightly tilted.

"I might have lived here once." I wink to keep things light.

"Recently?"

I nod.

"Why'd you move to The Jasper?" she asks.

"My business took off and most of my clients are in Manhattan, so it just made sense," I say so easily, so naturally, it scares me.

"Ah," Love says, taking slow steps as she examines the space around us once more. She doesn't question it, doesn't prod, and why would she? I've fed her nothing but lies from the moment we met.

"So what do we think?" The real estate agent slides her phone into her bag and struts our way in sky high heels that match her power suit and clack against the hard floor. I think I've seen her face on a park bench before.

Love turns to me, her mouth spreading into a wide grin. I nod, giving my silent approval, and she claps her hands together.

"I think I'll take it," she says, exhaling as her sparkling golden gaze snaps onto mine. "It's perfect."

"All right, let's all head back to my office," the agent says, strutting toward the door like we haven't got a minute to spare. "I'll just call my assistant and tell her to draw up the lease."

"You don't have to come with me," Love says, voice low as she leans close. "I don't want to take up any more of your time."

I check my watch, this one a leather-banded Burberry with a glare-resistant crystal that makes my trusty, waterproof Timex look like a child's toy, and press my lips flat as I pretend to contemplate my next move.

"Yeah. I've got a few things to wrap up this afternoon. And that conference call." I slide my hand in my pocket and glance at her. Love's enthusiasm radiates. I see it in her inability to stop smiling and the bounce in her step when she walks. I'm happy for her, and it's not bullshit happiness. It's genuine happiness because she's doing good things here.

"Thanks again for your help," she says. Rising on her toes, she leans in and air-kisses the side of my cheek—a complete 180 from last night.

Fuck. I think she just friend-zoned me.

Oh, how the mighty have fallen.

CHAPTER ELEVEN

LOVE

"SURPRISE!" My older sister, Cameo, stands at my door, her Chanel bag swinging from her left shoulder as her arms open wide.

"What are you doing here?" I ask, meeting her embrace and coming away covered in her abundant gardenia perfume. "And how did you know my new address?"

Cameo brushes her thick blonde hair from her shoulder and strides past me, placing her bag on my kitchen counter and taking a seat.

"Mom told me, silly," she says. "Anyway, the doctor and I are in town. He's got some kind of medical conference or something. We're flying home tomorrow, but I told him I wanted to spend the day with you."

"How is *the doctor*?" I ask, fighting a smile. I want to laugh every time she calls him that. He's a neurosurgeon back in Charleston, and Cameo takes every opportunity to remind us of that.

"Oh, you know, just doing his thing, saving lives one brain surgery at a time," she says, swatting her manicured hand. "Anyway, how goes it?"

Cameo rests her pointed chin on the top of her dainty hands, giving me her full attention. If I know my sister—and I do—she's hoping, maybe even praying, that I tell her I'm falling apart, that being a divorcee before the age of thirty is embarrassing, that losing Hunter has been the worst thing to ever happen to me.

But of course none of that is true.

"I'm doing great," I tell her.

Her head tilts. "Now, you know you don't have to say that just for my sake. I know you don't like people to worry about you."

"Seriously, Cam, things couldn't be better." I slide my hands into the back pockets of my Levis, wondering when Cameo's going to make a comment and pick apart my outfit. She's always been that way, critical and opinionated, always liked to point out my perceived flaws under the guise of being helpful.

Growing up, Cameo and I were never that close. We had more of an oil and water relationship, much to our parents' disappointment. Mom always thought since we were so close in age, we'd be best friends. But she didn't take into account that Cameo was born with a competitive streak a mile wide and the greenest envy I've ever seen in another human being.

Mutual resentment was the only language we spoke during our teenage years. Cameo hated that I ran track better than she could, she hated that I dated the boys in her grade that never gave her the time of day, and she hated that

I was a daddy's girl, but she never liked to go fishing and have coin tossing contests or any of the "boring" things Dad liked to do.

After Dad died and it was just us and Mom, we learned to put our differences aside and we got better at being cordial, but Cameo is still Cameo. Let's just say I love her, but only because I have to ...

And I think it'd make our father happy to see us together.

"Let's go shopping," my sister says, sliding off the bar stool. I'm not surprised that she doesn't ask for a tour of my place. Sometimes I think she's secretly afraid she might see something that will make her jealous, so she acts oblivious and disinterested. "The doctor gave me his AmEx and there's a Chanel store up the street. Need I say more?"

I've never understood Cameo's penchant for the finer things. We come from a staunch working-class family. Dad was a mechanic and Mom alternated between staying at home and working at the local bank as a teller when money was particularly tight.

Chanel, Versace, and Givenchy weren't even on our radar, let alone in our vocabulary.

"Give me a sec to get ready," I say before heading to my room to change. The saleswomen would have a fit if I walked in there like this. It'd be a moment straight out of that scene in Pretty Woman, and while I normally don't care what people think, dealing with dirty looks and Cameo at the same time might be a bit much.

A half hour later, we arrive at the Chanel on 3rd Avenue via taxi because my sister doesn't walk anywhere in New York.

"I need something to wear for the post-wedding brunch," she says, referring to her impending nuptials to *the doctor.* "Wedding colors are blushing gold and platinum, but I don't want to seem too matchy-matchy, so I might try to avoid anything pink."

A saleswoman with jet black hair and pale pink lips struts up to my sister and offers her assistance.

"Let me just pull a few things I think you might like, and I'll get a dressing room for you," she says before leaving.

Cameo and I take a seat on a white lacquered bench and she angles herself toward me, crossing her long legs.

"So," she says with a wicked smirk. "Any prospects?"

Arching a brow, I lean back. "Prospects?"

"Yeah. Are you dating anyone?"

"That's random." I glance toward the back of the store, wondering when the saleslady will be back to save me from my sister. "What makes you think I'm dating? The ink is barely dry on my divorce papers."

Cameo sighs, placing her hand on my knee. "I just want you to be happy."

"And I need a man to be happy?"

My sister laughs. "No. That's not what I meant. I just want to make sure you feel fulfilled in all areas of your life. Love is a very basic human need."

"I'm extremely fulfilled," I say, facing forward because I can't look at her right now. "Thanks for your concern though."

"You know ... if you ever thought about moving back home, the doctor's got a few single friends that I'd love to set you up with."

"Not moving back home." All of my memories of Sweet Water, West Virginia are tucked into the back of my mind where they belong, where they stay ideal and nostalgic forever, untainted by everything that's changed since I left for college at eighteen.

Once you leave home, it's never the same when you go back.

"You should at least visit a little more often," she says.

"I visit every other month."

When I first brought Hunter home, he couldn't get over how nice our town was, how friendly the locals were, and how clean and picturesque the tree-lined streets were. But after he made his first million, Hunter always found an excuse not to come with me to Sweet Water, calling it "hick-ish" despite the fact that he grew up in Ivy Grove, which wasn't half as pretty as it sounded. Most of his town looked abandoned, and the parts that didn't were filled with weedy yards and trucks parked crooked in gravel driveways after a night at the only bar in town. I always wondered if he was jealous of Sweet Water, resenting it for being quaint and homey and all the things he never had growing up.

"Maybe Mom should start coming here," I say.

Cameo clasps her hand over her heart, giving a bois-terous laugh. "I'd pay good money to see that."

I'm sure she'd waste no time slapping that on the doctor's AmEx ...

Mom's never been to New York, but she hates it anyway. She hates anything with crowds. State fairs. Theme parks. Concerts. Shopping malls on Black Friday.

"Anyway," my sister says, "we're finalizing the catering for the reception, and I really need to know who your plus one is and whether they want chicken or fish."

"Cameo."

"What?"

"I'm not bringing anyone," I say, my tone matter-of-fact.

Her jaw falls as if I've just blasphemed all over her wedding. "You know how bad that'll look? Everyone already knows about your divorce and if you show up alone, they're going to make a thing out of it, and I really want the focus to be on the doctor and me."

"I don't think people care about me as much as you think they do."

She rolls her eyes. "That's how it's always been, Love. And you know it."

"I thought we were past that." My voice tempers to a whisper. I don't want to get into it here.

"Past *what*?"

I don't buy her clueless act, and I'm not going to continue this petty and pointless conversation in the middle of a Chanel boutique.

"Anyway, we're less than three weeks out from the wedding so if you don't find a plus one in the next couple of weeks, let me know and I'll take care of it," Cameo says, inspecting her manicure.

Take care of it how?

"All right. It's ready for you," the saleslady says when she returns.

It's hilarious to me that she's hyper-worried about me stealing attention on her wedding day. I've seen her dress. It has miles of tulle and taffeta and a million beads. I highly doubt anyone could steal the show if they tried.

Although ... no one back home in Sweet Water has ever seen Jude Warner, and I can't help but chuckle to myself at the thought of showing up with him as my plus one. Talk about stealing the show. But I won't do that—to him or to her.

I turned him down when he asked me for a date. I'm not going to turn around and ask him to accompany me to my sister's wedding.

Cameo can protest all she wants, but I'm not bringing a date. Besides, I'll be too busy doing my maid of honor duties and ensuring she isn't freaking out at caterers and florists the week leading up to her dream wedding to *the doctor*.

"Love, come look at this," Cameo calls for me from the dressing room. "Do you think this blouse is too snug in the back?"

It fits perfectly. She's crazy. "It's fine."

My sister's matte red lips spread into a smile. "All right. I'll take it. But don't go anywhere. I'm going to try on a dress next. And when I get back, I want to tell you about this friend of the doctor's. You'll just love him."

Before she turns to head back into her dressing room, I say, "Oh? Did I not make myself clear earlier?" I feign ignorance. "I'm going solo."

"Do we have to talk about this right here?" she asks, her matching hazel gaze flicking to the saleswoman standing behind me.

Oh, *now* she cares.

"Nope," I say. "We don't have to talk about this at all because there's nothing more to say. I'm coming alone, and that's that."

CHAPTER TWELVE

JUDE

THE BAR OWNER licks the callused pads of chubby fingers and counts five bills, all of them hundreds.

"Here you go. Good show tonight," he says in a thick Jersey accent before giving my shoulder a squeeze. "Welcome back anytime."

I shove the money in my wallet and latch my guitar case before grabbing my phone and ordering a ride to the train station. It's a quarter past two in the morning and I'll probably get back to the city a couple hours before the sun rises, but this was worth it.

Singing with my guitar is the only time I feel like me.

The *true* me.

It makes me forget anything and everything that's bothering me. It's almost meditative because I'm so absorbed and in the moment.

I can't go the next six months without performing, so I

called around to a bunch of bars in Bergen County looking for work. The Green Elephant was the only place that called me back, and it was only because the band they booked had to pull out at the last minute. I had to audition via FaceTime and the guy mulled it over for all of five seconds before saying, *"You're hired. But ya gotta be sober and ya gotta play some covers. My people like covers. Bon Jovi. Guns-n-Roses. Ya know, stuff like that."*

My Lyft pulls up ten minutes later, and I load up in the backseat of a red Chevy sedan. The driver is a young woman, hair sunshine blonde and voice angel soft. She reminds me of Love, whom I haven't seen since we toured that building in Brooklyn a few days ago.

I keep wondering when I'm going to bump into her next, which means she's constantly on my mind. Love is the first thing I think about when I wake up and the last thing I think about when I go to sleep, and I've never experienced that with anyone before—not even the girl I dated for three years in my early twenties or the chick I dated for six months last year.

It makes no sense, but the more I try to fight my thoughts, the worse it gets.

I've given up trying to make sense of it, and all I can do is tell myself it could always be worse—I could hate her.

"We're here," the girl says as she pulls up to a train station. I grab my phone and tip her before climbing out and grabbing my guitar.

A few moments later, I'm buying my ticket and waiting by the platform for the 2:43 PATH train to Hoboken.

By the time I board, I settle into a seat in the back of the second car, hoping I'll have it all to myself so I can catch a quick nap. Resting my head against the glass, I close my eyes and try to fall asleep despite the dull ringing in my ears from tonight's performance, only the moment I do, all I can picture is Love.

Love laughing.

Love talking with her hands.

Love looking at me the way that she does, distracted and lost in thought.

This entire thing is fucked up.

Raking my hand across my mouth and exhaling, I push the thoughts from my mind and try to think about anything else but her: the Mets, the Killers, the Ramones, Piper and Ellie, Paw Patrol, Vinnie's Pizzeria. *Anything.*

If she knew who I really was, she'd want nothing to do with me—and rightfully so.

I can't fall for her.

I can't.

CHAPTER THIRTEEN

LOVE

"HEY, STRANGER," I call after Jude from our end of the hallway. He's just about to step onto the elevator, but he reaches out and holds the doors for me. "Thanks."

"Of course." His emerald gaze drinks me up and I realize the last time he saw me dressed like this, I was hidden under an oversized sweatshirt.

"Going for a run?" I ask, pointing to his Dry Fit shorts-and-tee get up before pressing the button for the main floor.

The doors close and it's just us and the scent of his shower-fresh skin.

"Thought I'd hit the trail in the park before that midday sun kicks in," he says.

"No consulting today?"

"Nah," he says, stifling a yawn. "Gave myself the day off. Was up late working last night."

We arrive at the lobby and he lets me out first, fingertips

grazing the bare skin on my back where my top has ridden up. My skin prickles at his touch, but I pretend not to notice.

Raymond watches us leave, giving us a nod and fighting a half-smile like he thinks he's witnessing the beginnings of something special.

"Hi, Raymond," I give him a wave. "How's it going?"

He gives me a wink. "Wonderful. Have a good one, Ms. Aldridge. You too, Mr. Warner."

Jude gives him some sort of wave-salute thing, and even as we leave, I feel him watching us.

"So nice out," I say, taking in a lungful of clean, mid-morning air.

Today is one of those rare summer days when it's not too hot, the breeze is just right, and the sky holds nothing but a handful of puffy white clouds that occasionally block the sun at just the right moments. Suddenly the idea of sweating it out at Soul Cycle while pop music blasts my eardrums doesn't hold the appeal of a jog in the park with a side of fresh air, but I don't want to invite myself along—he might get the wrong idea.

"You like to jog?" he asks, basically reading my mind.

"Uh, yeah, actually. I do." I stare ahead, tempering my excitement. Running in Central Park was one of the reasons I wanted to move to the Upper East Side.

"I could use a partner today," he says, one hand rested on his narrow hip, fingers tucked into the waistband of his shorts and a hint of taut skin peeking out. "Sometimes it gets boring ... going alone, I mean."

I hesitate, not wanting to seem desperate because I *am* desperate. Desperate for some fresh air and a sweaty, breathless, mind-clearing jog.

"I don't know ..."

Jude rolls his eyes. "Come on. Let's not do that thing where I invite you to do something and you hesitate and in the end, we both know you're going to give in. So ... just spare us both this time and give me that big, fat yes you're holding back."

I almost choke on my spit.

He's right.

And I didn't even realize I was doing it.

"You sure?" I finally ask, though I'm mostly doing it to mess with him.

"Good god, woman," he says, wrapping his warm hand around my wrist and leading me to the corner where we wait our turn for the crosswalk, and a few minutes later, we find a park bench and begin to stretch.

"Ready?" He jogs in place for a second as he waits for me to finish.

A moment later, we hit the trail.

I keep behind him a couple of paces, his strides being longer than mine, and I watch as the sweat gradually saturates his white shirt, making it cling against his muscled back. Halfway into our run, he pulls his shirt over his head and bunches it up in his hand, running all the while.

Two muscled divots down his lower back all but point toward his perfect ass, and I thank my lucky stars he doesn't know I've been staring at him the entire time we've been running. I've always found running to be a little boring with the exception of running track in high school, but I could run for hours if I had a view like this to keep me occupied.

Approaching a congested piece of sidewalk, we pass a couple of power-walking older women and a crowd of joggers and dog walkers when I lose him, but a minute later, I find him resting on the sidelines of the path, hands on his knees as he waits for me.

When Jude spots me, his olive-green eyes light in a way that Hunter's never did, and I feel it everywhere: in my bones, in my chest, in my stomach. I might not be dating Jude (or planning to), but I like spending time with him. Cameo would be happy to know that I find my time with him to be extremely fulfilling.

He joins up with me again, our arms brushing against each other as we navigate through a small pocket of tourists.

"Race you to that tree?" Jude says toward the end of our run. He points ahead to a giant oak surrounded by enormous boulders.

"What's in it for the winner?" I ask, words breathy and teasing.

"Winner gets to decide what we're doing Friday night."

I reach out, trying to jab his arm, but he dodges me in time. That whole quiet thing earlier was nothing more than me reading into him, worrying over nothing.

"Smooth," I say, pretending I'm more annoyed than flattered that he's still interested in me.

Jude turns back, flashing a quick wink. "So you in?"

He may have long legs, but I've got speed.

"Yep."

"Go!" Jude's strides lengthen and he's several paces ahead of me.

Clearly, I underestimated my competition.

Damn it.

Arms pumping and quads burning, I chase after him, catching up but not enough. The tree ahead grows nearer with each breathless second, and I'm so close I could reach out and touch Jude if I tried, but he's still in the lead.

A short moment later, his hand is splayed across the gnarled bark of the oak tree and he's wearing the biggest victory smile I've ever seen. As soon as I get there, he gathers me in his arms, securing his hands behind my back, and swings me around.

My skin sticks to his, the two of us glistening with sweat.

"You let me win on purpose, didn't you?" he asks, breathless and possessing a devious glint in his playful gaze. For a moment, it's just us. Everything else fades away for an endless second until he loosens his hold.

Waiting for my feet to hit the ground, I gently push him away. "That was all you, Daddy Long Legs."

"You almost had me a couple of times." He dabs his bunched-up t-shirt against his sweat-laced brow.

"Yeah, yeah, yeah." I rest my hands on my hips, trying to steady my breathing. "Head back now?"

Jude nods, and we make our way home to The Jasper quietly taking in the sunshine, the chirping robins, the rustling leaves, the gossiping nannies, the selfie-snapping sightseers, and the giggling children.

When we reach the lobby of our building, we wait for the elevator side by side, our hands so close they're almost touching. The doors part and we climb inside. I let Jude press button number seven.

"We should do that again some—" my comment is silenced with a kiss. One that comes out of nowhere. One that makes my stomach roll and my body weightless as the elevator lifts us higher.

He's backed me into a corner, my hands braced against the carpeted walls as my knees weaken.

His hands graze my jaw, his fingers tangling in the sweaty hair at the nape of my neck, and before I can protest, he kisses me harder. His lips taste of sin and salt. Lifting my hand to his hardened chest, I accept the dance of our tongues and I embrace the thrill of this moment—of being kissed by Jude Warner, who had to have me so badly he didn't care that I'm covered in sweat and my hair's a mess and there isn't an ounce of makeup on my ruddy, wind-kissed face.

I think he likes me.

And he likes me just the way I am.

The elevator doors open and the kiss comes to a gentle end as our eyes connect. Jude takes me by the hand, leading me toward our shared hallway.

We stop outside our respective doors, only this time we're not alone. The lady from the apartment next to mine steps out, squinting in our direction with a wrinkled stare. Even as she shuffles toward the elevator, her gaze is fixed on us. Whether she's nosy or entertained, I can't tell, but her heavy presence has served as a bucket of water on our fire.

"Give me your phone," Jude says.

"What?"

His palm flattens, inching toward me, and I retrieve my phone from the zipper pouch on the back of my leggings, handing it over. A moment later, he's programming his number into my contacts.

"There," he says, eyes smiling. "Now you can text me whenever you want to run again. Or, you know, whenever you want."

"You'd be so lucky."

He laughs through his nose. "You're right. I would."

CHAPTER FOURTEEN

JUDE

MY PHONE RESTS lifeless on my nightstand.

I gave Love my number yesterday after our run—or at least the number to the phone Hunter gave me, but she's yet to reach out. Every time I pass the window in the living room, I stop for a moment to watch the courtyard outside the main entrance, checking to see if Love happens to be coming or going.

I don't know what the hell she's up to today, where she is or who she's with or what she's thinking or if she's even remotely thinking about me ... and it's making me want her.

Really want her.

Not that it'd be hard to want her. She's fucking gorgeous. Kind. Fun. Great sense of humor. Doesn't take herself too seriously.

Jesus H. Christ.

I'm cataloging all of her qualities like this isn't all a giant, fucked-up ruse.

Grabbing my phone, I pull up a browser and do a little research on not-for-profit startups. I want to give her better advice, not that bullshit pull-an-answer-out-of-my-ass crap I gave her the other day.

From what I've gathered so far, it looks like she needs to draft bylaws and appoint directors. She'll need to hold a meeting of the board as well.

I click on another link to dig a little deeper into what kind of bylaws she might need for this place, only my screen turns black and Lo's name flashes across.

"What's up?" I answer, lying back against my pillow and tucking my left hand behind my neck. The state-of-the-art polished silver ceiling fan above me whirs, all of the blades blurring into one.

"Just checking in," she says with the permanent exhaustion of a young, single mother inscribed in her voice.

"Going well. Gave her my number today," I say. "Kissed her too. Since you're asking."

"Do you like her?"

"What kind of question is that?" I chuff.

"So that's a yes," Lo states, doesn't ask.

"Whether or not I like her has nothing to do with how this is going."

"It has *everything* to do with it," Lo says.

"She's cool. Yeah." My eyes squeeze shut and I massage my temples. It's way too fucking late for this kind of conversation.

"You like her."

"And you know that how? Because I said she's cool?"

"You're holding back," she says. "A lot. You do that

when you've got your guard up. And you only put your guard up when you're afraid of feeling something."

"How the hell are you only twenty-five?"

"You might be falling for her, Jude," Lo says, ignoring my question, "but she's falling for someone who doesn't exist. And once it's over, once she realizes what you did, there'll be no convincing her to take you back ever. Unless she's crazy. And in that case, maybe the two of you deserve each other."

Exhaling into the phone, I say, "Spare me the lectures for five seconds, please. They're getting really fucking old."

"You're getting defensive. You swear a lot when you're defensive. And you're defensive because you know I'm right."

"Wow, Lo. Sounds like you know me better than I know myself. Congratulations."

"Shut up," she says, half laughing but still serious. "Anyway, kind of sucks around here without you. It's too quiet. And the girls keep asking when Uncle Jude is going to give them their bedtime concert."

Dragging my hand through my messy hair, I smile, thinking about my nieces. On the nights when bedtime was more of a struggle than it should've been or my sister was working late, I'd grab my guitar and play them *Swinging on a Star* or *Baby Beluga* or a kid-friendly version of whatever Nirvana song was in my head at the time.

I miss my silly, carefree evenings with them, when I wasn't thinking about work or bills or how I flipped off the Wall Street-looking asshole in the Mercedes earlier that day for running a red light and damn near flattening a woman pushing a stroller.

Now chatty Moira Gutenberg who lives above us watches them the nights Lo works.

"I'll record some songs for them here in a sec and text them to you," I say, dragging myself out of bed and placing my feet on the silky rug that covers most of the floor and tickles my feet when I walk across it. Sure as hell beats the flattened, stained carpet of our apartment in Brooklyn.

Ending the call with Lo, I grab my guitar and take a seat in the living room, setting up the voice memo function on my phone and pressing record.

A minute later, I'm strumming the chords of *Buffalo Gals*—one of Piper's favorites. When I'm finished, I forward the memo to Lo and return to the app to record *Dream A Little Dream of Me* for Ellie, but a text pops across my screen.

The number isn't in my phone, but it's a local area code.

Pressing on the preview, a message fills my screen. "It's Love. Thanks for the concert. Just wanted to let you know that your voice is like a combination of Fergie and Jesus."

I laugh so hard, I snort. I can't believe this Fifth Avenue Princess just quoted *Stepbrothers*.

"Didn't realize the walls were so thin," I text back. "Either way, you're welcome."

"Why didn't you tell me you were musically inclined?" she texts, followed by, "What other talents are you hiding from me?"

"I speak fluent Russian and I play a mean kazoo," I reply.

"You lie."

A second later, I Google, "how to say *you caught me* in Russian" and then I text her, "*ty poymal menya.*"

It takes a second—I imagine she's looking up the phrase —but she responds with an entire string of emojis that suggest I'm a big fucking dork.

I know, Love ... I know.

A moment later, the little bubble fills her side of the screen before disappearing, and I realize I'm holding my breath and wearing a stupid grin on my face as I wait for her response.

I'm dying to know what she was going to say and why she deleted it and what she's going to say next. All of a sudden it matters to me, and I don't know why.

Shit.

Lo was right.

I think I'm starting to fall for Love.

CHAPTER FIFTEEN

LOVE

"EVER THINK about making a career out of music?" I begin to text Jude before deleting it. If I was still on speaking terms with Hunter, I'd send him that way in a heartbeat. He's exactly the kind of thing Hunter would piss himself for the opportunity to sign: a preppy, sexy Adonis with a golden voice, gentle but raspy in all the right places, *and* he plays guitar.

"Never got a chance to thank you for the run yesterday," Jude texts. "And for the kiss. God, those lips of yours ..."

I smirk as I contemplate my response.

He just had to bring that up, didn't he?

I begin to tap out a reply when my phone begins to ring.

"Hey, Cam," I answer my sister's call. "What's going on?"

"Just going over my pre-wedding checklist," she says, her tone somewhat breathy. I imagine her pacing the shiny

marble floors of the McMansion she shares with *the doctor*.
"How did your final dress fitting go? You know alterations
can take weeks sometimes. Did you give them my wedding
date? And you're still coming out a week early, right?"

"Final fitting is tomorrow," I say, keeping my voice calm
in hopes that it rubs off on her. "Seamstress can work with
the dates."

"Good, good. And did you book your room yet? The
block at the hotel is filling up," she says.

"Yep. Room is reserved."

"What about the bachelorette party? Have you started
planning that yet? I talked to Farrah and she said she hadn't
heard from you. Neither had Courtney," she says, referring
to two of the other bridesmaids. "They can take that off
your hands if it's too much."

"I've got it," I lie, biting my lip. My entire plan consisted
of forcing my sister to wear the gaudiest sash and veil I
could find and parade her around to all the bars on Sweet
Water's main drag like the show pony she loves to be.

"If you've got it, Love, then why haven't you sent out
invites? We're less than three weeks out," she says, pitch
rising. She's trying not to go off on me, but I imagine her
blood pressure is through the roof.

Good thing there's a doctor in the house.

"It'll be low key," I say. "I figured since everything else is
so proper and formal and fancy, maybe we could have one
night of small-town fun?"

Cameo makes some sort of groaning noise. Either she's
worried or she disapproves. Maybe both.

"You need one night to let loose and unwind," I add.

My sister pauses, mulling it over, before breathing into
the phone. "Fine. Just … no penis straws, okay?"

I almost choke on my spit. I've never heard Cameo use

the word "penis" before, and for some reason it's hilarious to me. That or I have the same sense of humor as a twelve-year-old boy tonight.

"You have my word," I say, holding back a chuckle. "No penis straws."

Jude.

I'd completely forgotten about Jude.

And now, I can't help but laugh because he thanked me for the kiss and I left him hanging ... I ghosted our conversation.

"You still there?" My sister asks.

"Yep, yep. I'm here."

She prattles on about the groom's cake next, how *the doctor* all but demanded German chocolate, but she finds it to be tacky and middlebrow, but within the same sentence she moves onto her future stepdaughters and how they posted a #tbt image on Instagram of their parents' on their wedding day twenty-some years ago.

I manage to appease her with the occasional and strategically dispersed "Oh, man," and "That's awful," and "Wow!" But after a solid ten minutes, I'm distracted by a quick knock at my door.

Slinking across the apartment, I peek out the spyhole and find Jude standing on the other side of the door, a pair of sweats hanging low on his hips and faded, gray t-shirt strangling his muscles.

As soon as I get the door, Jude begins to say something, but I lift my finger to my lips before showing him that I'm on the phone. Without saying a word, I wave him in and close the door.

He takes a seat on the couch, one dark brow raised as he studies my wincing face.

I mouth the word "sorry" to him and he sinks down into

my sofa, his legs slightly spread and his hands lifting behind his neck. He looks like he's got all the time in the world to wait for me to wrap up what could easily be a never-ending conversation.

"Okay," Cameo says, tone lighter than it was a moment ago. "Next order of business. Your plus one."

Rolling my eyes, I glance at Jude before saying, "No change there. Still just me."

"Okay, but ..." Cameo sighs, and I brace myself. I place Cameo on speaker because my hand is going numb and my ear is getting sweaty, "... who are you going to dance with? What are you going to say when Aunt Edie asks what happened with Hunter? Aren't you going to be bored at the reception?"

Composing a message to Jude, I write, "My sister called. She's getting married in a few weeks and everything's a matter of life or death right now."

Our eyes catch and his phone vibrates.

"I didn't know you had a sister," his types back, gaze flicking back to me.

I nod, pointing at my phone.

He returns his attention to his phone, tapping out another message: "You have a date for her wedding?"

"You sound exactly like my sister," I type, adding a sad face emoji before pressing send.

He smirks when he reads it, sending back a simple, "Ouch."

"Love, are you still there?" Cameo's tinny voice plays through the speakers. "I keep hearing a weird buzzing noise. What are you doing?"

"Yeah. Sorry. Cam," I say. "Can I call you tomorrow?"

"Everything okay?" she asks.

"Of course. I'll call you tomorrow after the fitting and

let you know how it went," I offer, hoping that will quell her stress a bit.

"Perfect," she says. "Bye, Love."

I end the call and return to my Messages app where a little red notification waits for me.

"Yes or no?" Jude's new text reads.

"No," I say outloud, placing my phone down.

He does the same.

"Do you need one?" he asks.

"No."

"Do you want one?" Jude's mouth twists and his eyes flash, and all of it makes my stomach flip without permission.

"Are you offering?" I ask him, though I'm not serious.

"I am."

"My family is nuts. I wouldn't do that to you," I say, rising. Heading to the kitchen, I connect my dying phone to its charger.

"Just so happens that I love weddings," he says, following me. "I'd love to be your plus one."

"You're a liar. No one loves weddings."

When I turn, I find him standing right there, so close, I can breathe in the musky clean scent of his muscled skin, and it silences me in an instant.

"I think ... Love ... that we'd have a really amazing time." Jude's voice is low, intimate, with just enough rasp to remind me of what his voice might sound like against my ear in the throes of the very thing I have no business doing with him. "So, what do you say?"

Surrendering to the smile on my face, I can't help but admit to myself that I've always enjoyed his company ... maybe a little too much at times. And I think he's right. We could have a good time together.

I'm not sure what it is about Jude that makes me cross every line I've drawn, that makes me push every boundary and barricade I've set up, but here I am, about to take him up on his ridiculously kind offer like a crazy woman with zero self-control.

"Okay," I say, exhaling his perfect scent from my tightened lungs. "You can be my plus one. But let me warn you … you have no idea what you've just signed on for."

But to be fair, I'm not sure I do either.

CHAPTER SIXTEEN

JUDE

HUNTER LEGRAND'S ASSISTANT, Marissa, escorts me to his office Monday morning. He'd texted me late last night, asking me to be here by nine AM sharp for a "progress report," which was shortly after Lo called me in tears and freaking out because she got a hospital bill in the mail for twenty-eight thousand dollars from the last time Piper was hospitalized with complications from her juvenile diabetes. I don't know why her restaurant even offers medical insurance to its employees when it's not much different than not having insurance in the first place.

"Would you like anything to drink, Mr. Warner?" Hunter's assistant asks, her baby blues fluttering and her tight floral dress leaving little to the imagination. Everything about her is fake … her breasts, her lips, even her eyelashes that look like thick strips of mink glued to her lids.

"No. Thank you."

She smiles. "All right. Well, Mr. LeGrand will be here any minute. Make yourself at home."

Marissa turns, her chestnut-colored ponytail swinging over her shoulder, and she closes the double office doors behind her.

This is the second time I've been in Hunter LeGrand's office, but the first time I've actually had a chance to do a little gawking.

Heading across the room to what can only be described as a "wall of accolades," I find framed and matted newspaper articles, photos of Hunter with various rock gods and music icons from Paul McCartney and JAY-Z to Chris Stapleton and Cardi B. In the center of it all rest his platinum records. I count twelve, all of them in the last handful of years, all of them on newer, lesser known musical acts who've gone on to massive overnight success. Hunter might be new to the music industry, but his reputation has quickly become that of a star maker.

Taking a seat in one of the onyx leather guest chairs, I cross my legs wide and glance at the gold-plated clock on the edge of his oversized mahogany desk. A cup of platinum pens emblazoned with Blue Stream's logo rests in a shiny gold cup next to his iMac monitor.

His office is boastful and unoriginal, everything I'd come to expect from someone whose Wikipedia page appears to have been written by the subject himself. I'd never seen anything so braggadocios before, so filled with the kinds of personal and specific things only those close to him would've known. His bio alone was twice as long as Dr. Dre's, and Hunter's only been around a few years.

The double doors burst open, damn near making me choke on my heart as it leaps into my throat, and Hunter LeGrand strides across his expansive corner office, his left hand smoothing down his black silk tie. Unbuttoning his gray suit coat, he hangs it on a gold rack in the corner before taking a seat at his desk.

"Jude," he says.

"Hunter."

"What do you have for me?" He leans back in his seat, the corners of his mouth turned down as he studies me.

"Everything's ... going well."

His frown deepens.

"Just ... well?" he asks, leaning forward and pushing a hard breath through his flared nostrils.

"It hasn't even been a month," I say. "We've been spending some time together, but I'm not going to come on too strong."

And I'm not a fucking miracle worker ...

Hunter's steely gaze flicks away for a moment and he does nothing to hide the displeasure in his groan. I didn't much care for this Napoleon-complexed douche the first time I met him, but now all I want to do is punch his stupid face and tell him to go fuck himself.

"Is Love being difficult?" he asks.

My nose wrinkles. "Love" and "difficult" don't even belong in the same sentence.

"Not at all," I say. "But this needs to happen naturally."

Hunter may be used to snapping his fingers or slapping down his AmEx and getting what he wants without having to wait, but his expectations are impractical here.

"Can I ask, why the six-month deadline?" I scratch my brow. "It just seems a little ... unrealistic."

"Unrealistic for a guy who's got no game, maybe?" Hunter says with a smug chuckle, adjusting his tie. His teeth are fake as fuck. Bright white, perfectly straight, and

obviously veneers. Imagining Love with Hunter is somewhat satirical to me.

He's so plastic.

She's so real.

"Insulting me isn't necessary," I say, stuffing my irrita-
tion down so I don't accidentally clock his ass.

"Take her to a romantic getaway or something," he says,
like the solution was so simple and right there in front of me
all along. "Women like that shit. Take her on a shopping
spree. I gave you that credit card for a reason."

"I'm actually going with her to her sister's wedding in a
couple of weeks," I say, "but as far as the shopping goes ... I
don't think she's into that. She doesn't seem that materialistic to me."

Hunter slaps the table and laughs. "You're going to
West Virginia? Have fun. And of course she's into material
shit. How do you think I kept her around so long?"

"I feel like we're not talking about the same person here
..."

His brows furrow, as if I've insulted him, but he
deserves it. The Love he described in that ridiculous binder
is nothing like the Love I've been getting to know.

The way he described her when he first prepositioned
me, made it a little easier for me to say yes. I'd walked out of
his office already of the opinion that she was a horrible
person and I was simply hired because Hunter was tired of
waiting for karma to do its job.

Their story isn't uncommon around here. Wealthy
Manhattan men get into ugly divorces all the time, losing
half their wealth or more, and their ex-wives walk away
with smugs on their Botoxed faces and enough money to
buy private islands and French chateaus many times over.

To a self-made man, I can understand how infuriating

that would be and how a man with little self-restraint and a bottomless bank account could be driven to actually go out and buy revenge.

"People change," I say.

Hunter's chin juts forward and he tilts his head to the side, like he knows I'm right, but he doesn't want to admit it.

"But back to the time frame here..." I continue.

He exhales. I knew he was trying to circumvent my question before. "What about it?"

"Even if she was madly in love with me, I don't think I could get her to marry me six months in," I say. "She's pretty level-headed, and she's not afraid to say no."

"Love?" He asks with a laugh.

"Yes. Love."

"Look, if you're getting cold feet about this, just say so. We can go our separate ways and forget this whole thing," Hunter says, rising and hunching over his desk. His gaze tightens, squinting. "Just remember, there are two very distinct paths for you here. The first path? All your dreams come true. You're a millionaire. You're famous. You never have to want for anything the rest of your life. The second path? You're right back where you started. You're some schmuck struggling to pay his rent and working dead-end jobs and playing in coffee shops and bars hoping to be discovered—but you'll never be discovered. I'll make damn sure of that."

My jaw clenches.

"Take her to fucking Vegas and get her drunk for all I care," he says. "Just ... get it done."

CHAPTER SEVENTEEN

LOVE

"WHAT'S her wedding dress look like?" Tierney asks from the seating area as I change out of my bridesmaid dress. Cameo will be happy to know it just needs to be hemmed. The seamstress said she can have it done in three days.

"You know those holiday Barbies?" I ask. "With all the tulle and lace and sequins?"

"Yeah?"

I tug my shirt over my head and fix my hair in the mirror of the changing room. "Like that."

"I'd expect nothing less from your sister."

Sliding into my cut off shorts, I zip the fly and fasten the button before grabbing my bag and the dress and stepping out.

"At least the bridesmaid dresses are cute," Tierney adds, eyeing the strapless rose gold number draped over my arm. "They're simple. That's good."

"Of course they're simple. She's terrified of being upstaged at her own wedding."

"With a Holiday Barbie dress, the only thing that could upstage her would be if Oprah showed up at the reception." Tierney rubs her belly, which seems to have doubled in size since I saw her the other week. "We almost done? I'm starving."

The seamstress returns to our area, taking the dress from me. When she turns to leave, she glances at Tierney and smiles.

"Looks like you're about to pop," she says. "How many weeks?"

Tierney's expression fades and she gives the woman a pregnant lady death stare. "Eighty-nine."

The woman's smile disappears and she clears her throat before walking away.

"I'm sorry. She's hangry right now," I call out, though I don't know if she hears me. I shoot Tierney a look, wordlessly trying to reason with her.

"You don't tell a pregnant lady she looks like a freaking elephant," Tierney whisper-yells.

Throwing my hands up, I can't say that I disagree. "You ready?"

She reaches for me, and I pull her up from the cushy velvet sofa she'd been waiting on ever so impatiently.

"Did I tell you I'm bringing Jude to Cameo's wedding?" I ask when we leave the tailor shop.

Tierney grabs my arm, her jaw dropping. "No. No you did not tell me you were taking Jude to Cameo's wedding. When did this happen?"

"We were texting the other night," I say. "It just sort of came up in conversation—the wedding did—and he asked if I had a date. And then he offered."

"That's ... amazing." Her hangry face turns into a wide, crazy eyes and an even crazier smile. "Good for you for getting back out there."

"I'm not 'getting back out there,'" I correct her using air quotes. "We're *just* friends and he's *just* my plus one."

"Whatever." She rolls her eyes. "Anyway, what do you think your sister's going to say when you roll in there with El Supermodel on your arm and she's walking down the aisle about to marry Doctor Saggy Balls."

"You're so bad." I bite my lip to keep from laughing.

"Seriously though ... Jude might upstage your sister at her own wedding."

"Plot twist."

Tierney laughs as we round the corner. The café she picked is only a block away, but I'm glad her sense of humor has been restored given her starving condition.

Before we reach the restaurant, Tierney takes a phone call from her husband, Josh, and I take a minute to check my phone. Pulling up my messages, I scroll down to Jude's name. The last time we texted was about Cameo's wedding. He's been quiet since then, giving me space I think. I love that he doesn't come on too strong. Intensity and persever-ance would turn me off. Hunter was intense. He wanted everything yesterday, and if that wasn't possible then he'd settle for one minute ago.

He rushed everything, always ... especially our rela-tionship.

We slept together the first week we started dating. Became exclusive by week two. By the end of our sopho-more year, he'd purchased me a gold ring with the tiniest diamond and proposed marriage, and within a month of graduation, we were officially Mr. and Mrs. LeGrand.

God, I was naïve then.

I didn't know anything about anything, and that included relationships. But I'm free now and I've never felt more alive or ready for whatever life throws at me next. I'm not that simple, trusting girl I used to be. I'm not that agreeable "yes" girl who put everyone else before herself.

I wouldn't even recognize my old self if I ran into her on the street.

Slipping my phone into the back-right pocket of my faded Levi cut offs, I follow Tierney into the café and try to pay attention as she rambles on about her baby registry, but all I can think about right now is Jude and how nice it would be to run into him again soon.

It's the strangest thing, but right now ... I kind of miss him.

CHAPTER EIGHTEEN

JUDE

THE DATE I "WON" fair and square is tomorrow night, and I've spent the better part of the evening trying to plan something that marries what I think Love would like to do with something from this ridiculous binder Hunter made for me.

Hunter claims her interests include the opera, fine dining (Butter and Tavern on the Green are her favorites), trips to the MoMA, French cooking classes, and wine tasting (he claims reds are her favorite despite the fact that I've only ever seen her drink white).

I can't picture Love doing any of those things, but the man was married to her for all those years. I doubt he pulled these ideas out of his ass, not to mention he wants this to work—*needs* this to work.

Rising from my living room sofa, I stretch my arms over my head and make my way to the kitchen to grab a bite. It's been storming most of the day, so I've been cooped up in this place, though I've reminded myself there are worse places I could be.

I'm elbow deep in the fridge, looking for something less frou-frou and more regular-dude, when the lights flicker and the inside of the thing turns black. Backing out, I realize my entire apartment is without power.

Heading back to the living room, I glance out the rain-slicked window to see most of our block is dark. Every window, every street light ... extinguished.

Collapsing across the sofa and wondering if it's possible to die of boredom, I realize I haven't talked to Love in a couple of days. I'd been giving her space, but I don't think it'd hurt if I confirmed that we're still on for Friday night.

The battery on my phone reads forty-three percent, so I should be good for now. Tapping out my message, I press send, place my phone on the coffee table, and wait.

Something like five minutes later (I tried not to count), she responds with, "Thought you'd forgotten."

My lips curl at the sides as I reply with, "Never" and then I add, "What are you doing right now?"

The bubbles fill her side of the screen for a few seconds before her message comes through, "Sitting in the dark, letting my face mask dry and doing some research for Agenda W on my phone."

"I've got some ice cream in the freezer about to melt," I text without giving it a second thought. "I'd hate to let it go to waste."

The sky flickers and a moment later, thunder rumbles the glass. I've always found storms to be sexy, provocative almost, with that hint of danger and satisfaction of being safely shielded. And if I'm going to sit in the dark, I'd rather sit in the dark with her.

"Keep the door closed. It should be okay," she writes.

I reply with, "I could. But I don't want to. So ... your place or mine? And mint chocolate chip or strawberry?"

Love sends me "Whatever" followed by "Yours. And strawberry. Just give me ten."

Sitting my phone aside, it finally hits me.

Sound Underground. That's where I'm taking her for our date. I think she'd like it, and it's different. It's this hidden bar you can only enter through the back of a Korean BBQ joint, and you need that night's password. Lenny, the owner, has an ear for finding the best budding talent, and he's discovered some of the biggest musical acts long before anyone else took notice.

Grabbing my phone and dialing the bar, I speak with Maureen, Lenny's wife of thirty-six years and dedicated personal assistant. A minute later, she puts me on the list and gives me the password for tomorrow's show: karma.

CHAPTER NINETEEN

LOVE

I WOULDN'T HAVE SAID yes, but I really, *really* hate storms.

Okay, I'm lying.

Maybe I would have said yes, but it's a lot easier for my psyche to blame this all on storms and not the fact that I secretly enjoy spending one-on-one time with my neighbor.

Hoisting myself up onto Jude's marble island, I watch as he retrieves a pint of strawberry ice cream and two spoons. A moment later, he props the softening carton open.

Flickering candles line the coffee table as well as the kitchen island, and I can't help but wonder if he lit them long before he started blowing up my phone about that stupid date he won or after he invited me over for ice cream? I honestly thought maybe he'd forget about the date, and I'd convinced myself I'd be okay with that, but I couldn't deny the small flip in my middle when his text came through earlier.

Swiping a spoon across the top, he hands it over, and I wait for him.

"Should we toast?" I ask, teasing.

"Do people toast with ice cream?"

Lifting a shoulder to one ear, I say, "Pretty sure you can toast with just about anything."

"If you say so." He digs his spoon into the melting pink cream.

"Should we toast to something specific or should we just toast?" I ask.

"I think most people toast to something specific, but you're the kind of girl who throws coins into fountains for no reason, so you could probably get away with toasting to nothing." Jude flashes a pearly smile that lights the dark and I clink my spoon against his his.

"There," I say before gliding the chilled metal between my lips.

When I showed up tonight, Jude answered the door in jeans and a t-shirt, his hair free from product and his skin barely scented with remnants of his morning shower. I think I almost prefer him this way—unbuttoned, undone, unpretentious. He isn't trying hard. Or maybe he isn't trying at all? Either way, it's working like some kind of reverse psychology trick on me because my heart is racing a million miles per hour and all I can think about is what his mouth tastes like.

"I have a question," I say, poising myself in his direction.

"Ask me anything."

"How can you act so laidback but look so hoity-toity?" I ask.

He almost chokes on his ice cream. "You think I look *hoity-toity*?"

"You're always dressed to the nines," I say. "And you work from home most of the time, so I don't get that."

"I have video conference calls sometimes," he says. "It's not exactly good for business if I look like a slob living in his mom's basement."

"Okay, but you don't have those *all* the time," I say, eyeing the way his jeans straddle the line between straight leg and skinny and fit him like they were personally sewn for his perfect physique. "I guess what I'm trying to say is ..."

What *am* I trying to say?

"I'm sorry. You remind me of someone else," I say. "Your style anyway. Not your personality. I even think you might wear the same cologne as him. I must associate those things or something."

Jude says nothing, listening as if this actually interests him.

"But you're so much nicer than he ever was. And you're authentic. That's something he never really knew how to be. Didn't realize it until much later, but everything about him was fake." I sigh, glancing to the side and remembering one night where he asked if I'd ever thought about getting breast implants "just to even things out a bit." And the fact that we'd just made love and his semen was literally dripping from between my legs only made the moment that much more cringe-worthy. "The world has enough fake people with their Instagram-perfect lives and their self-centered, ego-centric decisions. You're not like that, and I can't tell you how refreshing that is."

His lips press together as he nods, a small acknowledgement of my compliment, perhaps? And then his attention points toward the rain-beaded window in his living room for half a second. Jude's so humble, it wouldn't surprise me if he had a hard time accepting praise.

"So tell me about your family?" he asks. "Since I'm going to be meeting them and all."

"Sure you don't just want to be surprised?" I tease.

"Not really into surprises."

"Good to know." I lift my naked spoon and point it at him. "Neither am I."

"So you grew up in West Virginia," he says.

"Sweet Water," I say. "Little town no one's ever heard of ..."

I tell him about my mechanic father who passed unexpectedly of a brain aneurysm when Cameo and I were still in high school, I tell him about our little white house with blue door, about the mutt we rescued from the pound after Dad died. I tell him about my mother and her fear of crowds and how she's probably going to be high on Xanax for Cameo's wedding. And then I tell him about Cameo and her fiancé who's old enough to be her father and how she refers to him as *the doctor* instead of his name (Bob) because I suppose she thinks it makes her life sound better.

"What about you?" I ask when I'm done. "You said you grew up all over. What about your family? I know you have a sister. Do you have any others?"

Jude looks down for a second, placing his spoon on the counter with an easy clink. Drawing in a long breath, he says, "Nope. Just Lo and I. Dad's in prison. Mom's doing her own thing ... haven't spoken to her in years." His lips tighten and he offers a melancholy chuckle. "Our childhoods were night and day, Love. I'm afraid I don't have a lot of stories to share with you, at least none that wouldn't break your heart."

I want to reach for his hand, hug him, something. He's always been so cool and collected, but his voice is soft and his gaze is turned down, face wincing like he's recalling painful memories.

"So that's why you're so successful now," I say. "You saw how you didn't want your life to turn out."

He shrugs. "I'd hardly call myself successful."

"What?" I lean toward him. "You're insane if you don't think you are. You're educated and intelligent and funny and you own your own business. If that's not successful ..."

"Stop." He lifts his hand. "No more gushing. It's weirding me out."

At his request, I stop. If he doesn't want to hear how amazing he is, I have to respect that.

"Your ex," he says, changing the subject. "If he was such an ass, what'd you see in him?"

Sitting my spoon aside, I shrug. "He wasn't always like that. When I first met him, he was cute. Endearing. Really driven, which I admired. He had this ambition that just ... radiated off him, and I thought it was so attractive. It was a gift really. He was good at making things happen and that really worked out for him. But after he made his first million, he became someone I didn't recognize. And I was too far in, too convinced it was just a phase, to realize we were on the verge of self-imploding."

"You were blinded by love."

"I don't know," I say. "I think maybe we're always seeing what we want to see."

"It's human nature," he agrees. "Instinctual."

"What do you see when you look at me?" I ask. It's only now that I realize how close we are, how his arm rests on the counter beside my thigh and how the faded scent of his shampoo invades the space around me.

Thunder rattles the glass of the living room window, and it takes everything I have not to cling at his arm as adrenaline flashes through me. I've never loved storms, but I've always loved the earthy, musty scent that fills the air after a good rain. And I love being here with Jude, where there's chaos outside the window but peace and contentment in here. It's an exciting combination, and I want to remember this feeling forever.

Leaning back, Jude's head tilts and he studies me. "When I look at you ... I see someone I can't put in a box or a category. You're complex, but in a good way. I think you're still figuring yourself out, which is fine because I don't know any other twenty-somethings who have life figured out." Jude pauses, but I don't think he's finished yet. "There's this gentleness about you, like a canary who's been caged her whole life and now she's free and she's learning a new song."

I place my hand over my heart. My skin is warm to the touch, my eyes watering. I don't feel the thunder, don't see the lightening. In this moment, it's only him.

"That was sweet, Jude. Poetic, really."

Jude shrugs and thunder shocks the windows again. I place my spoon on the counter at the exact moment Jude is reaching for his and our hands graze, sending a spray of goose bumps up my arm.

I smile.

He smiles.

Maybe I'm imagining this, but I swear it's getting hotter by the second all of a sudden. Adjusting my posture, I brace my hands on the edges of the counter to slide down, but Jude rests his palm on my knee.

"Where are you going?" he asks.

"I'm hot," I say, exhaling and fanning my face. "Do you think it's hot in here?"

"Damn," Jude says, glancing across the room. "Thermostat says it's eighty-four in here. Guess no power means no AC. You okay?"

"Yeah. I think so." I'm in a strappy tank top and cotton pajama shorts. If I take anything else off, I might as well be naked.

Jude's hand reaches to the side of my face. "You're on fire, Love."

And it's not because I'm sick—that much I know.

"I'll be fine. What about you? You hot?" I ask, focusing on the way his t-shirt clings to his chest.

"A little." Reaching for the hem of his shirt, he gives it a tug. "You mind?"

My brows lift. "By all means."

I'm not sure why we're suddenly being so awkward and formal, but the runaway gallop in my chest leads me to believe that's all about to change.

CHAPTER TWENTY

JUDE

YANKING my shirt over my head, I toss it over one of the kitchen bar stools.

"Can't help but notice you're staring." I wink. "You like what you see?"

"*Stahp*," she says, swatting at me. Heat radiates off her delicate skin.

"Do you?"

"Who wouldn't?" Her brows center, like I've asked an idiotic question.

"Sure you're okay?" I ask, noting the way her cotton tank top clings even tighter to her body. One of the straps falls down her shoulders, and it's taking all the strength I have not to reach out and fix it. And good God, how did I not notice until now that she's not wearing a bra? Maybe it's built into her top? Or maybe it doesn't matter because all this means is she's comfortable around me. "You look ... really hot. And I mean that in all aspects of the word."

She brushes her hand against my chest and pretends to be annoyed, her eyes rolling to the back of her head.

"Fine. I'm hot. It's hot as hell in here. There. Happy?" Love fans herself, moving the wisps of blonde hair that frame her face before tugging at her top. A moment later she fixes that rogue strap, letting it snap across her shoulder.

"So do something about it." My mouth lifts at the side.

She feigns a scowl for a second, before her mouth twists upward. "If this is your way of trying to get me to kiss you again ... you're kind of taking forever."

My cock strains against my pants, an instantaneous response.

Was *not* expecting her to say that. I expected more coaxing, more flirting, more set up before the show.

"It's called the subtle art of seduction," I tease.

Reaching toward Love, I wrap my hand gently around her narrow wrist, depositing her hand on my shoulder as I position myself between her widened thighs. Her other hand slips around the back of my neck and her full lips arch.

Love is right. It's hot as hell in here. But the only heat I feel is the warmth of her skin against mine and ache between my legs that burns for her.

Love breathes me in. I cup her face, sliding my fingers into her soft hair. A second later, our mouths collide, and my heart is kick drumming in my chest, making me question the inauthenticity of this kiss on my end because it feels so fucking real.

Pressing her thighs against my sides, Love leans back, lifting her top over her head and tossing it aside, revealing her perfect teardrop breasts. Swiping my finger into the carton of melting strawberry ice cream, I lick the cool liquid off my finger before taking a pink budded nipple between my lips, swirling my cooled tongue around the pointed tip.

Love moans, so I do it again, blurring the sweet taste of her skin with the tang of sugared strawberries.

My cock hardens, straining against the inside of my boxers, but Love damn near reads my mind when she slides off the counter, reaches for my fly, and unzips me. A moment later, her hands are around my girth, pumping the length before lowering her pretty mouth to the tip and working magic with her velvet tongue.

Groaning and eyes squeezed shut, I bury my hands in her hair as she brings me to the brink.

And then she stops.

Glancing down, I realize she's standing before me, sliding her flimsy cotton shorts and pink satin thong down her thighs.

"What's this?" I ask, unable to wipe the championship winner's grin off my face.

"I think you know exactly what this is, Jude Warner," she says, her voice a soft yet confident whisper. No one's ever said my name the way she does—my full name—like she enjoys the way it feels in her mouth ... on her tongue. Bending, she trails the tip of her index finger down my chest then down the center of my abs before slipping beneath the loosened waistband of my jeans.

Fuck.

I can't take this anymore.

"Love," I say. She glances up at me from her position on her knees, her hand splayed on my Adonis belt, and she smiles. "I want you so fucking bad right now."

Pulling her up to a standing, I slide my hands around her hips and lift her until her legs wrap around me, and then I carry her back to my room.

Depositing her on the middle of my king-sized bed, I grab a rubber from one of the nightstand drawers, ripping the golden foil packet between my teeth. When I return to Love's side, she wastes no time tugging my boxes and jeans the rest of the way down—she's just as impatient as I am.

Sliding the condom into place, I move to the head of the bed and rest my back against a stack of pillows before pulling pull Love into my lap. Her arms hook around my shoulders as the sweet scent of her arousal fills my lungs and I cup her chin, pointing her mouth to mine before claiming it again. Reaching below, she wraps her hand around my cock and guides it inside her one slow, tantalizing inch at a time.

When I'm deep inside her, she offers the sexiest sigh I've ever heard and begins to pick up the pace, riding me faster, her nails digging into my back as she bites her full bottom lip.

Who knew sweet little Love Aldridge was such a sexpot?

This is completely unexpected, but watching her enjoy the hell out of herself only makes me harder, makes me want her more.

Gripping her hips, I press her deeper onto my cock, meeting her thrust for thrust so she can feel every inch of how hot I am for her. Our skin is slicked and sheened in sweat. Nothing about this is romantic—it's animal—but it's perfect.

I think she needed this.

And hell ... maybe in a way, I did too.

"You're fucking *dynamite*," I say to her, soliciting a smile that I waste no time kissing off those swollen lips of hers.

The thought of having this—having Love—all to myself

for the next several months and then never having her or anything this exciting again fills my mind, but I push it away, focusing on this moment and on this gorgeous woman who can't keep her hands off me.

Yesterday's gone. Tomorrow doesn't exist. All we have is right now, this calm before the storm.

CHAPTER TWENTY-ONE

LOVE

I WOKE up this morning to the hum of Jude's air conditioner kicking on, a kink in my neck, and a blanket covering my naked body. Sunlight poured through the window beside me as I sat up, finger combed my hair, and glanced around for any sign of life as last night played like a dream in my head. So perfect, so unreal. I wanted to close my eyes and relive it, second by second. The sound of the rain patting the window in soft drops, the feel of his skin, hot and sticky against mine, the warm, faded scent of his aftershave filling the damp air, the satisfying sighs coming from Jude's full mouth as he drove himself deeper into me ...

He'd left me a note on the bedside table.

Love,

Didn't want to wake you. See you tonight.

Jude

PS – Thanks for last night. Let's do it again sometime ...

But I'm home now, and while it's been almost twelve hours and a delicious, satisfying soreness still lingers between my thighs as I get ready for our date tonight. He hasn't said where he's taking me ... just that I should dress casually and comfortably and not expect anything fancy, which was a relief because pomp and circumstance gets old.

Spinning in front of my full-length mirror, I inspect my casual cotton shirt dress and tug a few face-framing tendrils from my messy top knot before stepping into a pair of strappy leather sandals.

This ... this feels good and natural to me.

Glancing in the mirror, I feel like I'm beginning to recognize the woman looking back at me for the first time in forever.

A knock on the door beckons me a second later, and I make my way to my next-door suitor who presents himself in jeans, a gray Ramones t-shirt, messy hair, and no glasses. He was dressed like this last night, only it was dark then, and I never really got to fully appreciate how amazing he looks like this.

He's all boy next door—literally—and one look at him sends a rush of blood to my head.

I'm dizzy with lust.

With his hands in his pockets, his eyes light when he sees me, and he bites his lip for a fraction of a second.

"Ready?" he asks, slipping his hand into mine with effortless ease, like it's the most natural thing in the world for him, and then he pulls me against him.

"Ready." I nod, and his lips graze mine before stealing a lingering kiss that leaves me weightless.

Breathing him in, I'm relieved when his earthy, mossy cologne is unfamiliar.

He doesn't smell like Hunter this time.

THE PLACE IS CALLED Sound Underground and Jude says it's secret, a word of mouth kind of place hidden behind a secret door in some restaurant in Chelsea. He knocks five times on a jade green-painted door that says "private" before a woman whose gray eyes match her hair greets us.

"Karma," he says, and she ushers us through.

Jude takes me by the hand, leading me through crowded tables before we get to one in the front row with a "reserved" marker on it.

"This is us," he says, grabbing my chair for me. I take a seat and he glances toward the busy bar. "What are you drinking tonight?"

"Um, surprise me?" I'm too distracted to concentrate on what I want to drink. The posters on the wall, the patrons shoulder to shoulder coming from every walk of life. Some with tattoos and piercings, some in business suits, some with rainbow-colored hair and wrestling singlets.

"I thought you hated surprises." His memory is impressive.

"Fine. Moscow Mule." I smile. "Thanks."

Jude returns a few minutes later, our drinks in his hands, and takes the seat beside me, scooting closer. By the time the opening act takes the stage, all the seats and reserved tables around us are filled with patrons, mostly the suit-dressed variety. I bet they're recruiters looking for fresh talent. I can't help but wonder if Hunter ever knew about this place. I can only hope he didn't. And if he did, I can only hope he's not here tonight.

The first song starts and Jude is laser-focused on the music, his fingers drumming on the table and his head bobbing ever so slightly. He's completely in his element, drawn in and intoxicated by this entire experience.

This is passion coming to life and it's sexy as hell.

I'm *so* having my way with him again tonight because as it turns out, Tierney was right. Sex doesn't equal dating.

And besides, a little fun never hurt anyone.

CHAPTER TWENTY-TWO

JUDE

I HAD to purchase a new suitcase, one with those fancy compartments where you can place your dress clothes without getting them wrinkled. A week's worth of every-thing is carefully packed, and Love's going to be here any minute.

It's been a week since I took her to Sound Underground and showed her a different side of me—the realest side of me. And when we got back that night, she wasted no time telling me exactly what she wanted me to do to her.

So I gave her exactly what she wanted.

Three times. Three different ways.

In the past seven days, we've jogged together like one of those annoying cutesy couples a handful of times, caught a couple of movies, and binge watched an entire season of *The Leftovers*, occasionally pausing the show because we needed to ... *take care of business*.

I can't keep my hands off her.

I don't know what it is, but I'm hooked. I'm addicted. I can't quit her. I've fallen and I can't fucking get up, nor do I want to.

I zip my bag just as Love knocks at the door.

"It's open," I yell.

A moment later, she steps inside, wheeling her bag behind her. "Car's going to be here in five minutes. You ready?"

"I am." I flash a smile. Spending a week with someone else's crazy family isn't exactly my idea of a good time, but a week with Love is, so it's a tradeoff I'm willing to make.

I lock up and grab her bag, wheeling both of ours to the elevator.

"Thanks again for doing this," she says after pressing the call button. "You're a saint. Truly."

I ignore her praise because I'm far from a goddamned saint. "So ... was going to ask you ... what do I say when someone asks who I am to you?"

The elevator arrives and we step inside. Love makes a gagging face. "Labels are stupid. Just tell them it's none of their business."

I smirk. "Seriously though. I can't say that to your family. What do you want me to tell them?"

Love presses the button for the lobby and shrugs. "Just say you're my friend."

The doors close.

"Is that all this is?" I ask. "A friendship?"

She turns to me, her liquid hazel eyes resting on mine. "Honestly, I've been having way too much fun to even think about what I'd call this."

We step off the elevator a moment later, and I follow her through the lobby and out the revolving door where we wait for our ride beneath the black awning outside The Jasper.

"We've been on several dates," I say. "We've had sex more times than I can count. And I'm not seeing anyone else ... are you?"

"No," she says.

"I'm pretty sure that means you're dating me."

Love's nose crinkles but her eyes shine. "Is that what that means?"

Releasing the handles of the bags, I slip my arm around her waist and pull her close. "That's exactly what that means."

CHAPTER TWENTY-THREE

LOVE

"YOU CAN PARK HERE," I say to Jude as we approach my childhood home in our rented Chrysler. For some insane reason, my palms began to sweat as soon as we got off the plane. I have no reason to be nervous, though maybe it has something to do with the fact that just a few hours ago, Jude informed me that I'm dating him, which means I'm about to introduce him to my family as the guy I'm dating, and I'm not prepared for their eleventy-million questions. Putting people on the spot is what my family does. They have it down to a science.

Unfastening my seatbelt, I climb out and eye the front door.

"It used to be blue." I frown as I try to determine if Mom painted it purple or magenta, because it's hard to tell from this angle and in this sunset lighting.

"What's that?" Jude asks as he comes around the front of the car and takes my hand.

"Nothing."

"You nervous?" he asks.

"Nope," I lie. "You should be though."

He laughs.

"I told you. My family wrote the book on crazy. Yours'll be a cakewalk. So relax," he says when we reach the front stoop. Turning to face me, he gives me a quick and proper peck on the forehead before we head in, so unexpectedly respectable it makes me laugh.

"Hello ... we're here," I call out once we're inside.

A cocktailed fragrance of fresh flowers, fabric softener, mint, and cinnamon potpourri wafts around in the same entryway I've traipsed through thousands of times before. We kick off our shoes on the same multi-colored rug Mom's had forever and I spot Jude leaning down to inspect a photo of my sister and me as gap-toothed kids posing with Mickey Mouse at Disneyland. Cameo's pouting because she has to share the spotlight with me and I'm grinning ear to ear, just grateful to be there because I'd waited my entire life (eight years at that point) to meet my idol.

"That her?" he asks, pointing to the pigtailed girl with tear-stained cheeks and folded arms standing a good foot away from a costumed Mickey.

"Yup."

"Awesome." He takes my hand and we share a smirk ... like he just gets it.

Voices trail from the kitchen, and judging by the cars parked out front, all three of my aunts are here as well as my Grandma Berta. And of course, I couldn't miss Cameo's shiny red Range Rover in the mix.

Heading for the kitchen, we find everyone gathered

around our old oak dining table, gabbing away while they have some sort of centerpiece assembly line thing going on. Over at the island, Grandma Berta is making mints shaped like wedding bells.

As soon as they notice us, the commotion stops and Aunt Edie shrieks.

"Love!" Aunt Edie pushes her chair out and waddles toward me, arms open wide and the familiar scent of Elizabeth Taylor's White Diamonds perfume wrapping around me. She squeezes me so tight I can't breathe and then she lets me go, only to hug me once more. "Look at you. I haven't seen you in years. How have you been? And oh, my, God, who is this handsome fellow you've got here?"

Cameo glances up, lace ribbons in her hands. Her expression hardens when she sees that I brought someone.

"Love," she says, her voice sugar-sweet. "You said you weren't bringing a plus one?"

Sitting the lace aside, she leaves the table and comes over to us. "Hi. I'm Cameo Aldridge, Love's sister."

"Jude Warner," he says. "Love's boyfriend."

Cameo's eyes widen and whatever she's trying to say seems to be caught on the edge of her tongue. Brownie points for Jude. No one's ever been able to make my sister speechless.

"Love?" My sister turns to me. "Can I talk to you in the next room for a sec?" She curls her finger and I follow her to the living room, trying not to laugh because she's about to spaz out. "You RSVP'd for one. We don't have a place setting for him. And what's he going to eat? Fish or chicken?" Pulling her phone from her back pocket, she shakes her head and presses her mouth flat. "I've got to call the caterer now and the wedding planner. We'll have to redo the seating arrangements at some of the tables."

"Cam." I place my hand over her arm. "Just relax, okay? He's really cool and laidback. He won't care where you put him or what you feed him. He's just happy to be here."

I sound like I'm describing a puppy.

Cameo exhales, her arms dropping to her sides.

"I know you're stressed," I say. "And I know you're sad that Dad's not here. But everything's going to be fine. Perfect probably. Knowing you. So just smile and let's try to have a good time and not worry about the little things, okay?"

She manages to smile before wrapping her lithe arms around my shoulders. The number of times my sister has hugged me I could count on two hands. Dad would be elated if he were seeing this right now—and I like to think he is.

As soon as she pulls away, she pats my shoulder and says, "Why don't you come and help make centerpieces?"

Just like that, she's back to her original form. My tiger-striped sister will never change her tiger stripes.

Heading back to the kitchen, I peek down the hall but I don't see Jude.

"Where's Jude?" I ask. I'm still not comfortable using the word boyfriend because this all happened so fast. I feel like a label like this needs to be broken in a bit, like new leather shoes. Maybe one day it'll feel natural. Until then, I'll refrain from calling him anything besides his given name.

"He's out on the patio with the guys," Mom says, wearing a dopey smile. She's either been hitting the Fuzzy Navel wine coolers or hitting the Xanax. Probably both. "They're smoking Cuban cigars."

"The doctor had them imported just for the wedding,"

Cameo says to my aunts. "They're engraved with our monogram."

"Oh, how nice," Grandma Berta says, though I'm not sure if she can even hear the conversation from where she stands.

I head over to say hello before making my rounds small talking with Aunt Clarice, Aunt Sheila, and Aunt Rosemary.

The patio blinds are pulled back, and from here I can see Jude standing outside, one hand on his hip and the other one lifting a thick cigar to his lips. If Hunter were here, he'd be in the next room, checking his email on his phone or making calls. Jude seems comfortable, at least from what I can tell from here. He's smiling and nodding and laughing and now he's talking, saying something to *the doctor*.

I hope he introduced himself as Bob Emsley and not "Doctor Robert Emsley the Third" or "the doctor." Bob is nice, but he can be just as uppity as my sister sometimes. It's why they're perfect for each other.

"So tell us about your boyfriend," Mom says. "We had no idea you were seeing anyone."

Neither did I.

Everyone stares at me, sending a quick flush to my cheeks. I haven't even thought about "our" story, how this all came to be. All I know is that I met him outside my apartment, he chased me, he caught me, and now here we are. Any other details I could share wouldn't exactly be rated G for General Audiences.

The patio door slides open and I glance up, making eye contact with Jude, who briefly bites his lower lip before smiling. My heart revs.

"Jude, why don't you have a seat," Mom says. "Cameo,

can you grab an extra couple of folding chairs from the garage?"

Cameo's jaw falls, as if my mother had just asked her to scrub toilets in her wedding gown.

"I'll get them," I say. When I return, everyone's laughing except Jude. He wears a polite smirk. "What'd I miss?"

"Your sister was just telling me about that time you were performing a clarinet solo in middle school and you fainted in front of the whole school and knocked one of your front teeth out," Jude says.

"It was hilarious," Cameo says, clapping her hands. "Bet you never knew she had a fake front tooth, did you, Jude?"

He looks to me, offering a wink. "Never would've guessed."

Jude comes toward me, taking the chairs from my hands and setting them up for us, and when I take the spot beside him, he rests his hand on my knee under the table and gives it a squeeze.

"There was this other time when Love was supposed to go on a date with this boy but she went to the wrong house because it was one of those streets where every house looks the same," Cameo says, waving her hand as she talks. "Anyway, she showed up at this house. The dad answered and said she was there for a date with their son. He tells her to come in and have a seat. A few minutes pass and out comes his son. Only it's Gerald Poppitt, literally the nerdiest kid in the whole school. Looked like a twelve-year-old, thick glasses, whiny voice. But Love was too embarrassed to admit she was at the wrong house, so she ended up going on a date with him."

"I wasn't embarrassed, I just didn't want to hurt Gerald's feelings," I say.

Jude nudges my arm. "That was really kind of you."

I can sense the weight of Cameo's stare, and I don't know why she's making it her personal mission to try to rouse up as many embarrassing childhood stories for Jude as she can, but I'm two seconds from shutting this down in front of everyone if she continues.

"Oh! Mom, do you remember that time Love—"

My lips part, but before I can begin to put Cameo in her place, Jude lifts his hand and just like that, it's as if he pressed the mute button I never knew my sister had.

"All due respect, Cameo, I think I'd rather hear these stories from Love," he says, "whenever she's ready to share them with me." He squeezes my hand under the table. "Did you guys know Love is opening a not-for-profit in Brooklyn?"

Cameo sits up taller, elbows on the table and hands clasped beneath her chin. "I wasn't aware, no."

"It's called Agenda W," I say. "I'll be helping women find jobs and eventually financial independence."

"Isn't that cute," Cameo says, returning her attention to the lace bows she's tying.

"I think it's pretty amazing," Jude says, turning to me.

Aunt Edie tells the group there's rain in the forecast for Saturday, and Mom clucks her tongue while Grandma Berta says rain on a wedding day is good luck and Aunt Sheila tells us not to get Cameo more worked up than she already is, which only serves to send Cameo flitting into the next room, leaving us to finish her centerpieces.

This is such a shit show and my crazy sister is center stage.

"So, Jude, what is it that you do for a living?" she asks. "You're in New York, right? I never did like the city."

"You've never been there, Mom," I say under my breath.

She rambles on, not giving Jude a chance to answer. "Too many people. All bumping into each other, yelling at each other. And I heard it stinks. I heard it smells like sewer gas, rotten eggs, and stuff. And everything's so expensive. Eight dollars for a cup of coffee, are you kidding me? They've lost their damn minds. I bet it's all that air pollution—what do they call that? Smog?"

Aunt Sheila shakes her head.

"You can't pay me enough money to go to New York," Mom continues, thin brows raised as she reaches for a roll of rose gold ribbon.

"You're really missing out," Jude says. "There's so much to do and see there. Some of the finest restaurants in the world are there. We've got museums. Broadway. Oh, and Love. She's there too."

I nudge him under the table. Telling her to come see me is a lost cause that I haven't fought in years. Once I almost got her to book a flight, but she asked if she could sleep on it and changed her mind in the morning. Carting her around the city and listening to her complain the whole time would be more work than it's worth.

Jude's underhanded remark goes over her head and she goes right back to talking about what a shithole Manhattan is.

"I heard they've got giant rats in the subways. And bed bugs!" She clasps the cross necklace dangling from her neck. "The whole city is infested with those disgusting things."

"Mom," I say, cutting her off so I can put her back on track. "Jude's a consultant."

"Oh, is that right?" Mom asks. Everyone turns to him. "What do people consult you for?"

"I specialize in strategic business consulting," he says. "Boring stuff."

"Oh, Edie, you know..." There goes Mom, changing the subject again. Or maybe she just needs to control the conversation because she needs something to control amidst all the chaos. "I ran into Carrie Ross down at the Wiggly Pig on Westwood the other day. You know her oldest just graduated from law school last month? Couldn't pass the bar. Poor thing is so upset. All that tuition money down the drain. He's going to try again, but can you imagine?"

"You want to go?" I whisper to Jude.

He shrugs. "It's your call."

Rising, I tell everyone we're heading out so we can get plenty of rest for the week. By the time we get back to the rental car, it's been a solid fifteen minutes. Quick goodbyes aren't a thing in my family. Someone always has to ask a question or chat your ear off so you can't get away.

"So," I say when we climb in.

Jude starts the car and fusses with the radio, tuning it to classic rock and adjusting the volume so we can still talk.

"You survived," I say.

He laughs through his nose as he backs out of Mom's driveway.

"You really had no faith in me, did you?" He reaches for my hand, bringing it to his lips and depositing a kiss as we head to the hotel.

"I was really set on coming to the wedding by myself," I say, watching how natural he looks behind the wheel of a car with one hand slung over the steering wheel and a relaxed expression blanketing his handsome face. Impressive for a city boy. He claims he had a car before he moved to the city, a 1987 Firebird with T-tops, and he's always kept his license current because he never knew when he was going to need it again. "But I'm kind of glad you weaseled your way into this."

He turns to me as we slow to a stop at a red light. "Weaseled? Is that what I did?"

"You know what I mean."

"I don't think I do," he says. "But feel free to show me just how *glad* you are as soon as we get back to the hotel ..."

He read my mind.

CHAPTER TWENTY-FOUR

JUDE

THE HOTEL DOOR opens Tuesday and I sit up, muting the TV. Love drags herself toward the bed, collapsing on the edge. She looks exhausted, but I know better than to tell a woman that. Besides, even as tired as she is from running around these last couple of days, she still looks amazing; messy hair, sleepy eyes, and all.

"Here," I say, scooting closer to her and rubbing her shoulders. "I've got you."

"I feel like I could sleep for a million years," she says, tilting her head from side to side as I massage her stiff muscles.

"Why are you doing all these things for her? Can't she delegate some of this stuff to other people? And doesn't she have a wedding coordinator?"

"All of her friends are fake and unreliable," Love says, "and she's my sister. She did the same things for me when I got married. Well ... not quite to this extent, but still. There's no one else."

"You're way too damn nice, Love."

She exhales. "I know. I'm working on that."

"You'll go crazy trying to please everyone." I kiss a trail up the side of her neck and she giggles. "But feel free to please me anytime you want."

Turning, she straddles me, her hands on my chest and sliding over my shoulders. "God, you're cheesy."

"You love it."

She kisses me, the shape of her grin pressing across my mouth, and another little part of me dies because I'd give anything for this to be real in a way that worked out for the both of us.

"Oh. Bob's bachelor party is this Thursday," she says. "Cameo wanted to ask me if you'd go."

"Isn't he too old for a bachelor party? What's he going to do, watch golf and drink single malt Scotch?"

"I didn't realize there was an age restriction on bachelor parties," she says. "Anyway, are you in or are you out?"

"Oh, I'm definitely in."

Love's hands hook around my neck and she leans in, grazing her lips on mine. "Thank you."

"For what?"

"For being you," she says, in a way that breaks my heart in two. "For everything."

Love collects the hem of her summer dress in her hands and tugs it over her head before reaching for my belt and her panties. Last night she was lying on my shoulder, her hand against my thrumming heart, and she told me she'd never been this voracious before, but I make her comfortable, I make her feel like she can let her hair down and enjoy this, and I'm the only man who's ever done that for her.

Love straddles me, reaching for the lamp on the side table and dimming the lights before grabbing a rubber.

"You have ten minutes until I'm out for the night," she says, flicking the gold foil packet and flashing a wicked smirk. "Make 'em count, Jude Warner."

Flipping positions, I pin her against the mattress. She's already exhausted, so I'm not going to make her do all the hard work.

Pressing my mouth against her hot flesh as I enter her, I can't ignore the weight in my chest. It's a reminder that I'm on a sinking ship. There's no life preserver. Nothing that can save me from the inevitable.

The more I get to know Love, the more I realize she's not the evil, money hungry, Park Avenue princess Hunter described to me.

She's ... *everything,* and even that doesn't fully encompass my opinion of this woman.

I've never known someone so sweet, so intelligent, so easy to be around. These last couple of weeks, I've all but smothered her and I haven't grown tired of her yet, which is a first.

The only thing I'm certain of is regardless of which direction this goes, I lose Love either way.

But that's exactly what I deserve, because I sure as hell don't deserve her.

CHAPTER TWENTY-FIVE

LOVE

JUDE STRAIGHTENS his tie in front of the full-length mirror on the back of the hotel bathroom door and I shamelessly ogle him. Cameo's big day is here—thank God—and after this, we can all move on with our lives.

"*What?*" he asks, meeting my reflection in the mirror. He's wearing his tortoiseshell frames and his hair is slicked. He's Fancy Jude today, but that's perfectly fine because Cameo's wedding is going to be "the grandest black-tie affair Sweet Water has ever known." Her words.

"Don't give me that. You know *what*," I say, biting the tip of my tongue. "I'd jump you right now, but I can't ruin my hair or Cameo will strangle me with her borrowed-and-blue garter belt."

Heading to the vanity, I steal a final spritz of perfume before rising on my toes and lightly kissing his cheek. Can't mess up my hair, can't mess up my makeup. The only reason I had to run back to the hotel was because in the chaotic rush of trying to make my hair, makeup, and nail appointments this morning, I forgot my phone charger.

"Can I be a total dog and say you look hot?" he asks. "I could say ravishing or something stupid like that, but I kind of feel like calling it like I see it today."

I smirk. "Wedding starts at two. United Church on 2nd Street."

"I'll be the guy in the back row who can't take his eyes off you."

"*Cheeeeeesy,*" I sing-song to him, trying not to laugh at his horrible one-liner. It's only then that I notice how sore my cheeks are. I haven't done anything out of the ordinary this week with my face ... that I can think of ... although I have been smiling much more than usual lately.

Yeah.

That's it.

━━

"LOVE, THERE YOU ARE," Cameo says when I arrive in the Sunday school room turned bridal party dressing room at the church, her voice sugar sweet. She's missing that crazy look that's been permanently etched in her hazel eyes all week. I don't know if she's on something or if her stress level is on its way back down since the end of all the wedding madness is in sight, but I won't question it another second.

Mom turns toward me, slowly smiling, her eyes unfocused. She's lit. I wonder how much Xanax she took this morning.

Cameo waves me closer. "Mom's doing my buttons, but I think they're crooked."

"Turn around." I examine the back of her dress, which is absolutely a hot mess of the bridal variety.

This morning started out with a light rain that cleared out just as we were headed to the nail salon, and just before lunch, Cameo's future stepdaughters, Tessa and Tiffin, informed the family they would not be attending today's nuptials. I don't blame them. Their father is getting married and Cameo made them *guestbook attendees*. She's never said so, but I think it was her way of being petty for all those times his daughters caused drama in their relationship.

Not my circus, not my monkeys.

I work the buttons as quickly as I can, undoing at least thirty of them before redoing them all.

"Where's the rest of the party?" I ask, wondering where the hell her so-called bridesmaids are. I know Cameo is difficult sometimes and she's one of those people you have to take in small doses, but her "friends" shouldn't have agreed to be in her wedding if they were just going to flake off the whole time.

I know Cameo is flawed and it's hard to be around her more than twenty minutes at a time without wanting to claw your eyes out, but at least she wears all her imperfections on the outside where we can see them, because most of us don't have that kind of courage.

Cameo forces a smile, but her glassy eyes say it all, reminding me that deep down under all that mascara and nail polish, she has a soul, she has feelings. "They're around here somewhere, I'm sure."

"There," I say a few minutes later. "Perfect."

Standing behind her, our eyes meet in her reflection. Cameo says nothing, just stares at herself. And as well as I know her, I can't even begin to guess what's going through her mind.

"You doing okay?" I ask.

"You asking me or Mom?" She points to our mother in the corner, passed out in one of the chairs, snoring. "Think she's still going to walk me down the aisle?"

Checking the clock on the wall, I realize the wedding starts in fifteen minutes.

"I'm sure Jude would do it?" I volunteer him.

Cameo shakes her head. "That'd be weird."

"Yeah. It would be. But I know he'd do it if you needed him to."

"He seems like a nice guy." Her compliment is breathy, like she's resolved to be happy for me. "You're happier with him than you ever were with Hunter."

My eyes widen. "Don't say that name on your wedding day. It's bad luck."

My sister laughs.

She draws in a deep breath, her bare shoulders caving in as she slumps forward. "This dress is so heavy. I've only been in it an hour and already my back is killing me."

"Just wait until you have to dance in that thing," I say, not that I speak from experience. My wedding to Hunter took place in a park, with hand-picked wild flowers and a simple white dress I found on clearance at Nordstrom Rack for eighty dollars. We were dirt poor but we were crazy in love. The wedding was all about us, not all the pomp and circumstance.

"Oh, sweetie, I'm changing into another dress for the reception," she says, waving her hand and scoffing. "That's what people do, you know, at *real* weddings."

Aaand she's back.

"Of course you are," I say. "I think someone just knocked?"

Grabbing the door, I spot one of the groomsmen

standing with a little Tiffany box in his hand. He must be pushing sixty, but he's got this sexy, George Clooney charisma about him. I'm pretty sure his name is Greg, and I'm pretty sure he's the one Jude said disappeared in the middle of the bachelor party Thursday night with some blonde he met at one of the gentleman's clubs they attended.

"A gift for the bride from the groom," he says.

"Thank you."

Shutting the door, I bring the little box to my sister, who yanks the white ribbon like she can't wait a single second more. Unclasping the box inside, she feasts her eyes on a platinum necklace engraved with her new initials in cursive.

Placing her hand over her heart, she turns to give me a closer look. "Isn't it gorgeous? He's the best."

I get it now: Cameo's love language is gifts, and so is Bob's.

And so was Hunter's.

Mine has always been quality time.

My sister is beaming now. Her quietude morphing into excitement that I can only hope is genuine. She's such a closed book sometimes ...

Three rapid knocks precede the wedding coordinator busting into the room. "All right, it's time. The rest of your girls are already out there waiting."

She's all smiles, and I try to imagine how anyone would actually want to do something like this for a living, but clearly she enjoys it because she still has a full head of hair.

"Mom, wake up," I say, tapping her shoulder until her eyelids flutter. "Time to walk your daughter down the aisle."

THE RECEPTION IS HELD in an old train depot in downtown Sweet Water complete with painted brick walls and at least twenty Swarovski crystal chandeliers. Now that the ceremony has ended, photos have been snapped, and we've taken the required limo drive for the past hour, we've finally arrived.

Heading for the open bar, I grab a glass of white wine and scan the room for my date. Er, the guy I'm dating? Whatever he is.

"Who does he belong to?" I heard a woman say to my left to her friend as she points.

Her friend cranes her neck. "I don't know, but I don't see a wedding ring ..."

Following their greedy gazes, I realize they're talking about Jude, who's currently cutting a rug to some Earth Wind and Fire Song. His partner? The six-year-old flower girl.

I let them finish their dance before cutting in.

"Hey," he says, taking my hand in his and giving me a spin as an Al Green song begins to play.

"Seems like you're having a good time."

"Told you. I love weddings."

"I see that," I say as he twirls me one more time. "Don't look now, but there are a couple of ladies at the bar that were, uh, noticing you a minute ago."

He looks anyway. Of course.

"Did you tell them I'm taken?" he asks.

"No."

"Why not?"

"Should I have?" I ask, nose wrinkled.

"Nah." He smirks. "Just thought it would've been funny, you getting all jealous."

"Never been the jealous type."

"Good. Me neither." He kisses me, something quick and appropriate in front of Bob and Cameo's hundreds of wedding guests, and then he pulls me against him, swaying to the music. The boy can dance.

I'm smitten.

Utterly, irrevocably, shamelessly smitten.

But still, as I dance the night away with this too-good-to-be-true Romeo who waltzed into my life when I least expected it, I can't help but wait for the other shoe to drop.

It always does.

CHAPTER TWENTY-SIX

JUDE

I WHEEL our bags to our apartments Monday night, just past eleven. With a wedding that spanned an entire weekend and a six-hour layover due to mechanical problems, I'm feeling like I could use a good, hard sleep.

Stopping outside our doors, Love yawns as she turns to face me.

"I had a good time," I say.

"You lie." She yawns again. "My family's insane. No one could possibly enjoy a straight week of their nonsense."

"Nah. They're more entertaining than anything else," I say. She hasn't begun to see crazy until she meets the rest of my family, and that'll never happen, so ...

Love's mouth pulls into a drowsy smile.

"That's putting it nicely." She closes the space between us, her hand splayed across my chest as she rises to kiss me goodnight. It's going to be weird sleeping alone tonight. I got so used to having her there. Her warmth and softness, her perfume clinging to the sheets and pillows. Waking up with her legs wrapped around me and her head tucked under my arm. If anyone else did that, I'd grab my shit and go sleep on a sofa, but with Love, I stayed put. And sometimes, through hazy eyes, I'd watch her sleep, listening to the soft cadence of her breath and smirking when she'd occasionally simper.

Love is peace and contentment.

Love is a soft place to land.

Love is a smile on my face when I wake every morning.

"Night," she says, backing away, head tilted as she looks at me like I'm the best thing to ever happen to her.

"Night." I watch her disappear inside her apartment, and god damn it, I miss her already. There's this void where she was standing a second ago. I feel it in the center of my chest, like a cannon-sized hole, and that means something.

I think I'm falling in love with her.

I can't do this.

I can't hurt her—not the way Hunter wants me to, even if it means sacrificing my dream and everything I've ever worked for.

Jabbing my key into my lock, I head inside, leaving my bag by the door and shuffling down the hall. Peeling off my clothes, I climb in a cold bed by myself, body succumbing to exhaustion but my mind running a hundred miles per hour.

Closing my eyes, I roll to the side and shove my hand under my pillow. I try to imagine how I'm going to tell her. How I'd start the conversation. Whether she'd break down in tears or hurl a crystal vase at my head. I try to imagine the things she'd say back to me—all of which I'd have rightfully earned.

But every scenario I dream up always ends the same way.

I thought I could do this.

And I committed myself to being a heartless bastard.

But at the end of the day, that's not who I am.

It's not who I'll ever be.

The man Love is falling for? That's me. Every quip, every kiss, every lingering gaze and cheesy line ... that's one hundred percent me. And the crazy thing is, she likes me in jeans with messy hair, drinking beer in a dive bar. The apartment never mattered to her. Neither did the bullshit consulting title or the pretentious wardrobe.

She likes me for me.

Rolling to my back, I exhale and pinch the bridge of my nose. I need to get some sleep. I need to gather my thoughts and figure out the best way to tell her—if there even exists a best way—because tomorrow? I'm calling this off.

Only there's one complication—Hunter had me sign a non-disclosure agreement.

I'm not allowed to tell Love about *anything* Hunter and I have ever spoken about, be it the weather or the intricate details of this arrangement.

All I can tell her tomorrow is that this isn't working out.

And that I'm sorry.

No explanation ... just an apology and a goodbye ... and after the incredible week we just spent together, she's going to be confused—rightfully so—and I'm going to walk away looking like an insufferable piece of shit—which I am.

I can only hope for her sake that this will feel like more of a sting than a sledgehammer to the heart. That maybe someday I'll just be that guy she dated briefly one summer, her memories of us fading with the years. And eventually she might even forget me, even if I couldn't forget her if I tried.

By tomorrow, Jude Warner and Love Aldridge will

become a thing of the past. A brief, passionate fling that was never meant to be. And I should have known from the start that War and Love don't belong together. They don't even belong in the same sentence.

She's all that is perfect and right in this world.

And I'm a destroyer, sent to demolish and ruin and devastate.

CHAPTER TWENTY-SEVEN

LOVE

THE BREAK in the curtain pulls me out of one of the deepest sleeps I've ever known, and in my half-awake stupor, I reach to the other side of the bed before realizing he's not there.

A persistent knocking echoes down my hall, again and again, over and over.

Smirking, I roll my eyes and step out of bed. It's probably Jude and he's probably going to surprise me with something ... breakfast in bed maybe? An early morning romp?

I bet he missed me last night.

I missed him.

We got home so late last night and we were so exhausted, we both decided to sleep in our own beds.

"I'm coming," I shout as I shuffle down the hall. A grin grows across my face as I reach the door and squint through the peephole. Only it disappears the second I see who's standing on the other side.

It isn't Jude.

Running back to my room, I grab a robe from my bathroom and cover my silky sheer pajamas before heading back.

A second later, I clear my throat and greet my ex-husband's assistant.

"Marissa, what are you doing here?" I ask, and I mean that in the most literal of ways. I don't know how she got my address unless Hunter gave it to her. "Did *he* send you here?"

"Can I come in?" she asks, worrying her full lower lip that looks even bigger than it was last time I saw her. Something about her looks different, and I realize she's dressed down today, leggings and a casual top, and her face is void of her signature caked-on Instagram-worthy look. She's absolutely stunning this way, so natural, but I won't tell her that. Once upon a time, we were friends and I convinced Hunter to hire her. But after the divorce, I never heard from her again.

Mulling it over, I release a held breath before stepping out of the way.

"I tried to stop by yesterday, but you weren't home," she says, a lanky arm resting on her hip as she stares at my floor. This isn't Marissa. I've never known her to be uneasy or uncomfortable, and I've witnessed her spending time around some of the biggest names in music without batting a mink eyelash.

"I'm so confused," I say, arms crossed. "Why are you here?"

"You might want to sit down," she says.

"If this is about Hunter, honestly, I don't care," I say. "I'm happy and I've moved on."

Her immense, round eyes flick into mine. "It's about that."

"About what?" I imagine him having me followed out of spite, just to check up on me, and I imagine him seeing me with Jude and growing insanely jealous because Jude is exactly the kind of guy who would bring Hunter's biggest insecurities to the surface.

"His name is Jude, right?" she asks.

I knew it. He's having me tailed.

"A couple months ago, this guy came in wanting to drop off a demo," she says. "Happens all the time, but this time Hunter was standing out there. He saw him and brought him back to his office for a meeting. That never happens. You know that. It's just not how it works."

"All right." I cling to her every word.

"Anyway, they were talking and he must have hit the intercom button or something because I could hear everything on my headset, and normally I'd disconnect, but at first, I couldn't believe what he was saying."

"What? What was he saying, Marissa?"

"He told Jude," she says, pulling in a deep breath. "He told him that if he could get you to marry him, he'd give him a record deal and some cash. A lot of cash."

I think I'm going to be sick.

Ambling toward the living room, I brace myself on the back of a chair.

"Please don't tell them I told you," she says. "I signed a non-disclosure with Blue Stream, and I don't want to lose my job, but I just thought you should know that you've been set up."

The room spins and I manage to find my way into the

chair. Eyes closed tight, I imagine all of these moments with Jude … the fountain … the elevator … Brooklyn … the kiss … the jog … the week in West Virginia … all the sweet and wonderful things he said … the way he looked at me like I meant something to him, truly meant something.

"I'm so sorry, Love," she says, coming to my side and placing her hand on my shoulder.

I don't even cry. There isn't so much as a hint of tears brimming in my eyes.

In fact, I feel nothing.

No. I take it back. I feel like a fool.

"How do I know *this* isn't a setup?" I ask. I imagine Hunter having me followed, seeing that I'm happy, and then trying to sabotage that. The day the judge ruled in favor of the alimony request, I'd never seen such rage flash in his eyes as he glowered across the courtroom at me. But I only saw it for a moment before my attorney shielded me and his attorney got him the hell out of there.

Marissa shrugs. "I can't prove anything. I only know what I heard."

It all seemed so real, *felt* so real.

"Hunter set him up with apartment close to you. Bought him new clothes. Gave him a credit card and a phone," she says.

An image of Jude in glasses and a suit fills my mind first. Whenever he was dressed up, he was always so proper, so mysterious. But when he started coming around in jeans and mussed-up hair, he'd let loose a little more. And it makes sense if he's a musician, because he took me to that Sound Underground place to hear some up-and-coming band.

It all makes sense to me now, why there were two very different sides of Jude Warner.

"Please don't tell them I told you," Marissa asks again, hands clasped.

I lift a hand, my head beginning to throb. "I won't say anything."

"Jude came by a few weeks ago," she says. "I didn't hear the conversation that time, but he had this look on his face when he left ... I don't even know how to describe it other than he looked ... worried? But maybe I was reading into it."

The room won't stop spinning every time I close my eyes, so I try and focus on the gold paperweight resting on a stack of books on my coffee table. I need to concentrate on something that means nothing to me, something incapable of ripping my beating heart clean out of my chest.

"Do you want some water or something?" she asks. "You look like you're going to throw up."

Waving her away, I feel a spasm deep in my belly. "Can you just ... can you leave, please?"

I've heard enough.

Marissa says nothing as she trots toward the door and shows herself out, and the moment the door slams behind her, I run to the bathroom just in time to empty the contents of my stomach.

Reaching for a towel, I dab at my mouth, the very mouth Jude kissed a million and one times over the past month, and I begin to retch again. Only this time, my stomach is empty. Much like the hole that now resides in the space that once held my heart.

The faint sound of my phone vibrating across my nightstand somehow manages to steal my attention, and I stumble out of the bathroom to grab it.

But I stop cold when I see the name on the screen.

"Are you up?" his text reads.

Falling for him was so easy, so effortless. Now I know

that was only because he was doing a job. He was being paid to make me like him. He was paid to be perfect and to say all the right things.

Disgusted doesn't begin to cover the way I feel about Jude now.

Another text comes through, "Let me know when you get up. Or just head over. I'll leave the door open for you."

"Fuck off, you sick bastard," I say out loud. And then I power down my phone and flip it over.

I need to decide how I'm going to handle this ... because I *will* handle this.

CHAPTER TWENTY-EIGHT

JUDE

IT'S BEEN twenty-four hours since I texted Love Tuesday morning, and now I'm beginning to worry because she's never gone more than a few hours before responding. Half of me wants to call the super to check on her, to make sure she didn't slip in the shower or choke on something, but I was in the hall earlier, and I swore I could hear the TV going in her place.

I was ready to stop this insanity yesterday.

Most of Tuesday was spent pacing my apartment, mentally running over all the things I was going to say to her over and over again—which wasn't some big long monologue by any stretch of the imagination, but I'd managed to work in some words of comfort.

Maybe the week together was too much? Maybe things were going too well and that scared her off?

Regardless, I grab my phone and call her.

"Hi, it's Love. Leave a message," her sweet, gentle character is inherent even in those six little words.

"Love, call me," I say after the tone. "Please."

All this time we've spent together and not once did she ever seem like the kind of person to hold a grudge or cut someone out of her life for no reason. And the last time I saw her, she kissed me.

She kissed *me*.

Thumbing through my contacts, I find Lo and give her a call. I need a reality check. A kick in the ass. Something.

"You were right," I say after she answers.

"Duh," she laughs. "But right about what, exactly?"

"Everything." I hook my left hand around the back of my neck as I stand next to my living room window and gaze out at Central Park.

"You fell for her."

Sighing, I say, "Yeah."

"Then I think you know what to do," she says. "Tell her the truth, back out of this, and come home. You made a shit decision, and now you have to man up and deal with the consequences of that."

"I was going to tell her everything yesterday," I say. "But she won't take my calls or return my texts."

"Seriously?" Lo asks. Ellie babbles in the background mixed with the sound of Paw Patrol blaring on the TV. "Do you think ... do you think she found out?"

"God, I hope not." I wanted to be the one to tell her. Figured I at least owed her that.

"Maybe it's nothing. Maybe she's sick or something? Who knows. Just ... I guess keep trying her?"

It's not like I have any other option.

"And Jude," Lo says, "I know you did this for the girls and me. And I know you're just a good guy who did a bad thing. But I wish you'd stop feeling so responsible for us. You'd be just fine if you didn't have us three weighing you down. I'm tired of being a burden on you, and I can't help but feel like this whole thing was partly my fault."

"Lo ..."

My entire life, I've looked after her without a second thought, and not once have I ever thought of her as a burden. Even as kids, I was always protecting her, making sure she was fed and had clean clothes, walking her to school and chasing off anyone who so much as thought about screwing with her.

All we've ever had is each other, and when she had the girls and wound up completely on her own—homeless, essentially—taking them in wasn't even a question.

"You're not a burden, you're *family*," I say. "As soon as I get out of here, I'm going to take the first job I get. I'm going to book extra gigs on the weekends. And you're going to start nursing school."

In this moment, I can't help thinking about Love's charity and her mission to help women become financially independent.

Love ... this multi-millionaire who could easily spend her time jet setting around the world and lavishing herself with designer bags and real estate ... wants to make it her life mission to help people exactly like my sister.

If that doesn't tell me what kind of person she is, I don't know what does.

She's got a heart of gold.

And I'm about to shatter it into a million fucking pieces.

CHAPTER TWENTY-NINE

LOVE

"THREE WORDS," Tierney says over the phone the next day. "Fake. Pregnancy. Test."

"T ..."

"I'm serious. I can pee on a stick for you, get you a positive, and you can scare the bejeesus out of him," she says. I can just imagine her pacing her apartment, auburn brows twisted and hand waving wildly as she talks. Everything sets her off lately. I call it her pregnancy rage, but I don't dare call it that to her face. I'm hopeful that after the baby's born, she'll be back to her calm, yoga-and-green tea-loving self. "I hate him, Love. I *hate* him. What a fucking ... ugh."

I don't disagree with her.

"What are you going to do? Just keep avoiding him? Ignoring him?" she asks.

"I don't know." I hid in my apartment all day yesterday, worried I might run into him before I had a chance to decide how I was going to handle this, but I can't hole up forever. I thought maybe a good night's rest would help clear my mind by the morning, but all I did was toss and turn because my mind refused to shut off. All I did was replay every little moment, every hand hold and gentle touch and lingering glance.

I still can't believe none of it was real.

"You need to beat him at his own game," she says. "Take karma into your own hands."

"I don't know. I don't think I have it in me to be that cold and calculating."

"You don't have a choice, Love. What he did was the most selfish thing I've ever heard of. He makes Hunter look like a saint, and that's no easy feat."

"Nah. They're in the same boat as far as I'm concerned. Hunter put him up to this."

"Still," she says. "You need to feel vindicated so you can move on from this asshole, and I'd really like to keep the whole fake pregnancy test option on the table."

I chuckle, almost snorting tea through my nose. "No. That's psycho girlfriend territory, and that's a line I refuse to cross."

Tierney sighs. "Oh, Love. Always keeping it classy."

Taking a seat in an oversized living room chair, I turn sideways, draping my legs over the arm as I cup my hands around a mug of steaming Earl Grey. Outside, the city is just beginning to come to life. Horns are honking. Birds are soaring. Joggers are jogging.

"You know ..." Tierney says, "What if you give him exactly what he wants? Come on strong, pretend to be crazy in love with him, make him think his little scheme is working? And then when he proposes to you, say yes ... and then leave him at the altar?"

"You don't think that's a bit extreme?" I ask before immediately deciding I'm not touching that with a ten-foot pole.

"Honey, what he's doing to you is extreme. An eye for an eye."

I laugh through my nose, covering the phone. She *really* needs to have this baby.

Taking a sip of tea, I mull it over. The numbness waned off late last evening, bringing on a rush of anger and sadness. I thought maybe everything would feel a little less intense when I woke up this morning, but nope. If anything, my anger has intensified, taking shape in the form of a pounding headache and a jaw that won't unclench.

I still have yet to shed a tear over that bastard, so there's that.

"It felt so real, Tierney." I release a soft breath, glancing at the spot on the sofa where we first made love—or rather, when he first fucked me.

I'd burn the stupid thing now if I could.

It's tainted, only serving as a reminder of what a moron I was.

"Of course it felt real," she says. "That's what he was hired to make you believe."

"I wonder if he ever second-guessed what he was doing? Do you think he ever felt bad about it?"

"Doubtful. If he did, he would've stopped."

"True." I lift my mug to my lips. I can't help but wonder if there's the slightest chance he was catching feelings for me, but I don't say anything to Tierney because I know what she'll say. And in the end, it doesn't matter.

I'll never be able to believe a word he says ever again.

"I should go," I say, sliding my legs off the arm of the chair and placing my mug on the coffee table.

"What are you going to do?" she asks.

"I'm going to text Jude and see if he's home," I say, "and then I'm going to beat him at his own game."

Ending the call, I pull up my Messages app and fire off a text. It shows read instantly, like he's been waiting for me to respond, and within seconds he replies, telling me to come over and that the door is unlocked.

The queasy fuss in my stomach that hasn't subsided since Marissa gave me the news only intensifies, as if my body is firing off warning signs. But the more I think about this, the more my anger focuses on Hunter just as much.

Jude was a pawn.

A heartless pawn.

But Hunter is the real mastermind behind *all* of this.

I'd love nothing more than to let him think his clever little plan is working and then pull the rug out from under him. And if I really wanted to go all out, I could get my attorney involved. I'm sure hiring a guy to marry your ex so you can stop paying alimony isn't one-hundred percent legal, and if there's a loophole, my legal counsel will find it.

"Give me an hour. XOXO," I text him before heading to the shower.

My entire life, I've always taken the high road.

But screw that.

I think it's time Jude Warner discovers what it's like to be a pawn in someone else's game.

CHAPTER THIRTY

JUDE

SECURING a towel around my waist and wiping the fog off my bathroom mirror, I think about Love for the millionth time since I woke up this morning. And truthfully, I haven't stopped thinking about her once since we got back. I'm fixated. Obsessed. Torn and tortured. And I have no one to blame but myself.

My phone buzzes next to the sink and a little white notification pops up.

LOVE: Are you home?

My heart stammers, and my stomach is weighted with that sinking feeling I've had since I made my decision.

I want to see her ... but seeing her means ending things ... which means I'm never going to see her again the second she walks out my door.

I text her back, "Come on over. The door's unlocked."

LOVE: Give me an hour. XOXO

I sit the phone aside and stare at my reflection, brows furrowed, forehead lined. How she could go from ignoring me for twenty-four hours to texting me like nothing happened is beyond me, but I'm sure there's an explanation somewhere. I've never wasted my time trying to figure out the intricacies of the finer sex, and I'm not about to start now.

My lungs tighten as I finish getting ready. Smooth shave. Crest. Antiperspirant. Cologne. Clean clothes. It's any other morning ... except it's not.

The threat of a knot builds in my stomach, but I try and focus my attention elsewhere. Grabbing my phone, I play a little Bob Dylan.

Growing up, when Mom and Dad were having one of their knock down drag-out fights, I'd always take Lo and hide in my room, lock the door, and crank some Bob. His music was so otherworldly, so unlike anything else out there, that it always seemed to take us away, somewhere else where our dad didn't beat our mom and our mom wasn't drunk twenty-four-seven and our house didn't have cockroaches and the electricity wasn't getting shut off every other month.

Wagon Wheel comes on first, which historically has always managed to put some semblance of a smile on my face, only this time it never comes and I don't find that temporary escape. I'm still here. Still staring at the reflection of a douchebag who sold his soul ... for nothing.

The next hour passes in a hazy blur.

I've paced my apartment countless times, practicing what I'm going to say to Love and exactly how I'm going to say it. I've pictured tears in her honeyed eyes and trembles on those sugared lips, but imagining heartbreak playing out on her face will have nothing to seeing it in person.

The palpitations in my chest quicken when I hear the twist of the door knob and the soft pad of footsteps across my foyer.

"Jude?" she calls.

I make my way from down the hall, breath resting in my chest because it hurts too fucking much to breathe, and when I round the corner, I'm met with the widest smile and brightest hazel eyes I've ever seen.

Before I get a chance to say anything, she's leaping into my arms, wrapping her legs around my waist and pressing her strawberry-flavored mouth against mine. When she pulls away, she's still grinning.

"Where have you been?" I ask, focused on the killer smile I'm going to miss like hell when it's gone.

"I'm so sorry," she says, smile fading as she slides off me. Her hands wrap around the nape of my neck, her fingernails lightly dragging against my skin. "I woke up yesterday with a horrible migraine—I get those sometimes—and the only way I can deal with them is by taking one of my pills, turning off my phone, and shutting out the world until it goes away. I slept all day. I'm so sorry. I would've told you, but it hurt way too much to even look at my phone. Forgive me?"

Dragging in a deep breath, I press my lips flat and nod. "Of course. I was just worried, that's all."

"Let's go do something. I want to get out for a bit." She stretches her arms over her head before turning and walking back toward the door. Stopping, she glances back at me, waving her hand. "Come on."

"Where are we going?"

Her shoulders lift and she smiles. "I don't know? Anywhere. I just want to be with you. I don't care what we're doing."

My feet are still planted, my mind fixated on how and when I'm going to end this with her. The thought of that beautiful smile vanishing sends a shock of literal pain across my chest. And I sure as hell can't have this talk with her in public.

"What?" she asks, half-laughing. "Why are you just standing there staring at me like that?"

Love hooks a hand on her hip, her nails still painted the same shade of dusty rose that she wore all week for the wedding, and I'm instantly taken back to the night of the reception, dancing until the very last song when her feet were so sore she had to carry her heels, but she refused to stop because she said it was one of the best nights of her life.

Dragging in a ragged breath, I run my hand through my hair and shrug.

One more day.

I'm a selfish bastard and I want one more day of this.

One more day to hold her, to hear her voice, to kiss those berry soft lips.

Love moves to my side, slips her hands gentle around mine, and pulls me toward the door. I grab my keys and wallet from the console in the foyer and follow her out the door. As soon as I'm finished locking up, Love wraps her arms around me from behind. The sensation of her cheek pressed against my back as her arms hold me tight nearly takes my breath away, and when she finally releases me, I turn to face her.

"Overcompensating much?" I ask.

She smirks. "Just making up for lost time."

"It was just one day." I pretend it didn't matter to me, that I didn't spend every waking second of those twenty-four hours wondering about her.

"Didn't make me miss you any less." Love slides her

hand into mine and we head for the elevator, and within minutes we're strolling along Fifth Avenue hand in hand like it's any other summer day.

We pass one of Love's favorite coffee shops and she pulls me inside, ordering my usual before I have a chance to protest. Caffeine is the last thing I need. I already can't sleep as it is.

"Thanks," I say, taking the iced coffee from her hands. "You didn't have to do that."

"It's the little things, Jude," she says. "And you're the one who's shown me that."

"I have?"

Her golden-brown gaze locks onto mine as we walk and the corner of her mouth lifts. "Why do you act so surprised? You're always doing things for me. You're probably one of the most selfless men I've ever met."

A lump lodges itself in my throat, but I swallow until it subsides.

"It feels like a dream ... being with you." Love slides her dainty hand into the bend of my elbow and sighs. "And I never want to wake up."

I keep my eyes trained ahead. I don't have to look at her to know she's smiling. Her exuberance is palpable, radiant and more blinding than the sun. Leading her on for another twenty-four hours would only be adding another layer of cruelty to this shit sandwich.

"Love ..." I say, chest tightening as I try to force the words out. For a second, they get stuck, and I have to take a moment to breathe, to compose my thoughts. "Could we go some—"

The pull on my arm tells me she isn't paying attention, and a second later, she's dragging me into some pop-up museum called *The Future Is Now* on 77th.

"I've been hearing about this," she says. "Everyone says it's amazing. Want to go?"

We're already here ...

"Sure," I say. Love leads me inside, and I get us two tickets at the front desk and the woman behind the counter offers us two headsets for the self-guided tour.

We spend the next two hours immersed in futuristic technology and displays of what scientists are predicting life to be like in the next twenty, fifty, and hundred years as the pre-recorded tour guide explains what we're looking at.

Toward the end of the experience, Love yanks her headset off and slides my arm over her shoulders. I pull my headset down, resting around my neck as she looks up at me with sparkling eyes full of life.

"I love this stuff," she says. "I love thinking about what comes next. All the possibilities ... all the different directions we can go." Love exhales, resting her cheek against my chest. "Anything is possible, right?"

Clearing my throat, I concur. "Right."

"I don't know about you, but this place gets me *really* excited for the future."

CHAPTER THIRTY-ONE

LOVE

JUDE'S FINGERS rake through my hair as I lie in his lap, a throw blanket pulled up to my shoulders. We're catching up on The Leftovers at my place and every so often, I find myself forgetting that this isn't real because it feels like it did before.

But the truth changes everything.

And the truth doesn't let you forget for long.

Glancing up, I study the underside of his chiseled jaw before lifting my hand to cup his face. As soon as he feels the warmth of my palm, he glances down at me, smiling, but there's something missing in his eyes.

He's been quiet today. Withdrawn.

We started out with a coffee and an impromptu trip to a museum followed by brunch and a matinee before heading back to my place to cool off once the afternoon sun took full effect.

The shades are drawn, the lights are low, but he hasn't so much as tried to make a move on me. Last time we tried watching this show together, we had to stop and rewind the show halfway through every episode because we were so focused on each other that we weren't paying attention to the storyline.

Maybe I'm coming on too strong?

Maybe he thinks he has to pull back a little and keep that perfect equilibrium between us in order for his little scheme to work?

"One more?" he asks when the credits begin to roll.

It's the third episode we've watched today, and I'm beginning to get sleepy from sitting in a cool, dark apartment all afternoon, but I nod.

I'm going to smother him with togetherness.

After all, that's what he wants right? He wants me to be smitten with him, to be madly in love, to never want to leave his side until *after* he walks me down the aisle.

Halfway into the next episode, my lids are anchored and I'm fighting to stay awake. Jude's fingers stroke lightly through my hair, tickling my scalp, and it all but puts me in a trance. Allowing my eyes to close, I succumb to the gentle nap that's been calling my name since I first lay down.

Turns out pretending to be someone you're not is exhausting and the day is finally catching up to me.

I wake to the sensation of Jude's arms scooping beneath my shoulders and lifting my limp arm around his shoulder. I'm not sure how long I've been out, but a slitted glance toward the windows shows me it's already night.

"Shh," he says.

"Why are you carrying me to bed?" My voice is soft, half of me still planted in a dreamlike state.

He says nothing, only deposits me on the left side of the

mattress, tugging the covers up to my chest and adjusting the pillows behind my head.

"Are you leaving?" I ask, growing more awake by the second.

My room is dark, and all I can make out is the shuffle of Jude's feet against my hardwood floor, followed by the soft rumple of clothes falling.

"No," he says, almost whispering. "I'm not going anywhere."

A moment later, he slides in beside me, the heat of his body making its way to me before he does. When his arm slinks around my stomach, he pulls me against him. His skin is hot to the touch, his breath warm on the back of my neck. Our bodies meld together, forming a perfect S where every part of him is cemented to every part of me. And then he holds me tighter. Tighter than before. Like he doesn't want to let me go.

In this still, small moment, I can't help but wonder how much of this is fake.

CHAPTER THIRTY-TWO

JUDE

I DIDN'T SLEEP a minute all night.

I couldn't.

I lay there, watching Love the entire time. Soaking up our last night together, replaying the perfectly low-key day we spent and how she never left my side.

I wanted to tell her yesterday, but every time I tried, something thwarted my efforts or she was looking at me in a way that made it impossible for me to break the news right then and there.

I put it off and put it off until the opportunity slipped away and the day turned into night, and then I carried her to bed. I was going to leave because I wasn't sure if she was going to want to make love or not, and I wasn't sure I'd be able to. To go from wild, passionate sex to dumping her the next morning isn't something I could ever bring myself to do to her.

I go over everything in my head for the thousandth time.

You're an incredible woman.

Any man would be lucky to be yours.

You've made me happier than I've ever been with anyone else.

But you deserve better.

I wish I could tell you more, but that's all I can say and you're going to have to trust that this is for the best.

I'm never going to forget you.

And I'm sorry that it didn't work out for us—sorrier than I could ever put into words.

I hope someday you can forgive me, and that you can find someone who makes you feel as wonderful as you always made me feel.

The sunrise peeks through her bedroom curtains, and she stirs, rolling toward me. Her eyes are still closed, her expression still peaceful and lax. As if she can sense me watching her, Love's mouth curls. A second later, her eyes squint open and she reaches, hand slowly extending toward my cheek.

"I think I'm in love with you, Jude Warner," she whispers before letting her hand fall to my chest. Love shifts closer, nuzzling into my arm with a soft sigh.

I keep quiet, watching as she falls back asleep, waiting for her breathing to steady.

If things were different, I would tell her.

I would tell her I think I'm in love with her too.

CHAPTER THIRTY-THREE

LOVE

HE'S GONE when I wake, and the alarm beside me reads a quarter past eight. When my blurred gaze comes into focus, I spot a little slip of paper folded next to the clock.

LOVE,
    Went for a run. Didn't want to wake you ...
    Jude

TOSSING the note back where I found it, I drag myself out from the heap of covers and press my bare feet against the floor. It's odd that he didn't invite me ... we *always* run together.

Regardless, I try not to read into it and instead head to the shower to get cleaned up for the day. When I'm finished, I grab my keys and wallet and run out for coffee and bagels. He's always starving after he runs, so this will give me a chance to show up and show out as the besotted woman he believes me to be.

Twenty-five minutes and a milelong line out the door later, I'm strolling down the sidewalk, arms full of breakfast, when I spot a familiar face up ahead.

A heavy glug fills my stomach and I glance around for an opportunity to avoid the inevitable, but before I get a chance to make a move, he's already standing in front of me.

"I'm going to have to call you back, Drew." Hunter pulls his phone from his ear, stopping in front of me, and it's only then that I spot a pretty young thing on his arm, her baby face covered in five layers of Instagram-worthy makeup. Her arm hooks into his as she studies me with an unapologetic curiousness, and from the corner of my eye, I catch the glint of a giant rock on her left ring finger. "Love."

I don't say anything at first. The last time I saw him was after the alimony ruling and now ... knowing what I know ...

"You can say hi, you know," he says, his mouth drawing into an enchanting smile, one I know from experience to be fake. "It's good to see you. How have you been? Oh, this is Maleenia, by the way."

Maleenia ...

I'm pretty sure I've heard of her. If I'm not mistaken, she's some twenty-one-year-old Yugoslavian pop star wannabe with over three million followers on Snap Chat.

Of course, he's engaged to her.

In fact, I wouldn't be surprised if *she's* the one whose graphic text message I received the night my marriage imploded. Guess all it takes to win over a girl like Maleenia is a few dick pics and the promise of a record deal.

"Really?" I ask. My brows rise and I ignore the young

woman. If I didn't spend the better part of the last half hour standing in line, I'd toss this coffee all over his YSL button down.

"Really, what?" Hunter plays dumb, which only makes me clench the brown paper bag in my left-hand harder.

"You're just going to pretend everything's fine?"

He lifts his hand to his jaw, glancing away as he chuckles. "Love, we're grown adults. Let's act like it."

"Wow," I say. "Not even married anymore, and you still can't speak to me without your signature condescension."

"Love ..." His head tilts as he studies me, and for a moment, I can't help but wonder if he's missing me or patting himself on the back for making the right decisions. Either way, it doesn't matter. "I'm sorry. I just ... we're going to be running into each other from time to time, and I don't want it to always be so strained. That's just not healthy."

"I see you've been talking to Dr. Kissinger?" I ask, referring to the marital counselor we were ordered to talk to when we first filed our legal separation.

Talking or fucking. Probably both.

The woman had this Machiavellian look in her violet eyes during each and every session, like a cougar waiting for the right moment to pounce on her prey, and she did nothing but guide us toward divorce the entire time, saying it was her professional opinion that we had both changed and grown too much over the course of our marriage to make it work any longer.

But that's neither here nor there.

"I'm sorry, Love," he says, uttering a word I'd never once heard him say before. "I'm sorry it didn't work out. I just wish you the best. That's all."

No. He doesn't get to take the high road. He doesn't get

to have the last word and walk away looking like a hero while I stand here feeling like a jaded ex-wife.

He doesn't get to do that.

He doesn't get to make *me* feel like the one with a chip on their shoulder.

Hunter begins to walk away, but I can't help myself.

"Apology accepted," I call toward him, forcing tenderness into my voice and a smile on my lips.

He stops, turning back to face me, eyes squinted as he searches mine. What is he looking for? Honesty? The man wouldn't know honesty if it smacked him across the face.

"I'm sorry it didn't work out," I say. "But I have to tell you ... I really think everything happens for a reason."

"Of course. I couldn't agree more."

"Actually, it's funny because, I've met someone recently," I say, glancing up at the cloudless sky for two seconds as I release a contented breath. "And he's amazing. It's so strange, it's like he just ... came out of nowhere. And he's everything I could ever want in someone. Perfect for me. Eerily perfect. And I never would've met him if we were still ... you know."

Hunter's eyes light.

Either he thinks his plan is working, that his freedom from alimony is just around the corner.

Or he reads between the lines and realizes that I know exactly what he did.

Either way I win because as soon as I get the chance, I'm going to make sure that rug is pulled out from under him so hard, so fast, he won't know what hit him, and all those things he fought so hard for with his cold, dead heart will be forever out of reach.

Just like that.

"Speak of the devil," I say when I spot Jude up the sidewalk.

He's shirtless, his smooth, tanned body glistening with sweat under the morning sun, and I manage to wave him over.

Hunter turns to follow my gaze, and then he watches as Jude sidles up to me and kisses the top of my forehead.

"Hey," I say, rising on my toes to kiss his salty, minty mouth like I'd done so many times before.

The two of them exchange looks for a brief second but avoid eye contact after that, each of them focused on me and me alone.

It feels unnatural playing the two of them. I've never been a manipulator and it feels akin to wearing tight, dirty clothes. I want to take them off and change into something clean, something better fitting, but all's fair in love and war.

"Hunter, this is Jude," I say, realizing I haven't technically introduced them yet. "Jude, this is Hunter. The ex-husband I told you about."

I watch Hunter's eyes flash for a moment. He hates when anyone talks ill of him behind his back, but what does he expect? Jude glances down at me, one brow raised like he's confused. And he should be. Now that I think about it, I haven't ever said much about Hunter to Jude. I've only ever referred to him as someone I once knew.

"Anyway, we should get going," I say, eye snapping onto Jude's. "I got us breakfast. Thought you'd be hungry after your run."

"Jude, good to meet you," Hunter says, though he doesn't extend a hand. Jude nods, and my ex focuses on me next. "Love, hope to see you again sometime. Take care."

With that, he's gone, and I unfasten myself from Jude's side.

"I didn't realize you were still friendly with your ex," he says while we head back to The Jasper.

"Is that a problem?" I respond with a question that doesn't confirm nor deny what he's asserting.

"Not at all. You just never talked about him much. I assumed you weren't on speaking terms."

I'm not sure why he's asking me this or why it matters, but the way his forehead is lined and his jaw is tightened, it seems like he's genuinely curious.

"Actually," I say, "this is the first time I've seen him since our divorce was finalized. He was surprisingly cordial."

"You didn't expect him to be?"

I laugh. "I didn't. He's not a good person, Jude. He was a terrible husband. He lied, he controlled, he cheated. Our divorce wasn't pretty."

Jude is quiet, lost in thought perhaps, and by the time we make it to our lobby, he still hasn't said a word.

I can only hope he's finally seeing Hunter for who he is. I hope it makes him realize he fucked up. And from here on out, I hope it keeps him up at night, eats away at him and makes it hard to look himself in the mirror every morning.

We ride in silence to the seventh floor, and when we make it to our hallway, I hand over his coffee and breakfast.

"I've got some meetings today," I say, checking the time on my phone. "Need to finalize the logo for Agenda W and stop by my attorney's office to sign a few more things, but I'll be around tonight …"

Jude's olive gaze searches mine, only now he's looking at me differently.

Closing the gap between us, I hook an arm over his shoulder and rise on my toes before pressing my mouth against his. The kiss is quick, less than passionate.

I don't understand what's happening.

I'm giving him everything he wants and he's pulling back.

"Can I see you tonight?" I ask. "When I get back?"

Worrying the inside of his bottom lip, he says nothing.

"Jude?" I say his name, half-chuckling. "You okay?"

"You told me you loved me this morning," he says.

Is that what this is about?

Does he think I love him and he's all of a sudden growing a conscience?

"I did?" I play dumb.

"You were half-asleep," he says, "but you said it ... did you mean it?"

Lifting my shoulders, I tilt my head and smirk. "I said it, didn't I?"

"Love ... did you mean it?" he asks again.

"Why would anyone say something like that if they didn't mean it?" I ask, leaning close and kissing his mouth again. "I should get going. I'll text you on my way home later."

He stands there watching me as I walk away, cooling cup of coffee in one hand and the brown paper bag in the other. I don't stay long enough to study his reaction, though by the time I'm back inside my place, I almost wish I had.

Not that it would make a difference.

The damage has been done.

CHAPTER THIRTY-FOUR

JUDE

SHE *LOVES* ME.

I mean something to her.

This is more than the beginnings of a summer fling that never quite got off the ground.

I rinse the soap from my body and kill the shower water before grabbing a towel and wrapping it around my waist. The glass on the mirror is fogged, but it's all the same because I'm the last person I want to look at.

I knew ending this was going to be messy, but Love's admission adds another layer to an already complicated situation.

I can't keep this going.

I can't drag this out a second longer.

Grabbing my phone from the bathroom counter, I dial the number for Blue Stream Records. Hunter's assistant answers on the second ring, placing me on hold. As soon as she returns, I tell her I need to meet with him immediately.

"He's out of the office right now," she says, "but he should be back soon."

Yeah. I know. I ran into him an hour ago.

"I could put you in around eleven, if you'd like?" she offers.

"I'll take it." I give her my name and end the call, struggling to drag in a single humid breath in this stifling bathroom.

Today's the day.

———

"I DON'T UNDERSTAND." Hunter perches on the edge of his polished desk, his fist pressed against his frowning mouth. "I saw you two this morning. She looked happy. You had your arm around her. And now ... *now* you want to pull the plug? Are you fucking *kidding me*, Jude?"

Hunter's shaky gaze lock onto mine and his thin lips are fused.

I knew he'd be angry.

I knew he wouldn't shrug his shoulders and say, "Okay!" and send me on my way.

"I don't expect you to understand," I say, keeping an eye on his clenched fists and tight posture and the fact that he's looking like he's two seconds from clocking me—not that I couldn't handle the pipsqueak.

"Are you ... did you ... do you *love* her? Is that what this is about?" His nose is wrinkled, the tone of his voice snarled. "You caught feelings for her and now all of a sudden you've grown a fucking conscience?"

Yes.

That's exactly it.

"No," I lie. It's none of his fucking business how I feel about Love.

"Then what's the problem?" Hunter slides off his desk and paces his expansive office, stopping to take in his million-dollar view. His silence concerns me, but it doesn't scare me. I've already made the decision to sacrifice everything I've ever needed in my life so that Love doesn't have to. "That hard part's over. Why would you walk away when you're so damn close?"

"She doesn't want to get married again," I lie again. "It's a lost cause."

"Bullshit."

"I don't want to waste her time. Or mine," I say, "or yours."

"Bull-fucking-shit." He turns to me, brows pinched. "She's the most malleable human being I've ever known."

"Maybe she was when you were married to her," I say, "but that's not the impression I got."

Hunter strides to his chair, collapsing into the seat and burying his head in his hands as he exhales. He mumbles into his palms, something I can't discern, and when he finally glances up at me, he leans back and throws his hands in the air.

"Fine," he says. "You don't want to finish this? That's on you. I can't force you to do something you don't want to do. But I just want to remind you that you signed an NDA. You can't tell Love *anything* you and I have *ever* spoken about."

"Well aware."

"You're going to have to break it off with her immediately," he says.

"That's the plan."

"And I want you out of that apartment by the end of the week."

"Not a problem."

"You can never see her again," he says. "Do you understand that?"

Releasing a hard, steady breath, my gaze snaps onto his. "Yep."

Hunter rises, smoothing his tie against his flat chest. "And don't you ever go looking for a record deal—here or anywhere else. You're dead to this industry."

It's all the same because without Love, I'll be dead inside too.

CHAPTER THIRTY-FIVE

LOVE

"I CANNOT BELIEVE you dropped the L-bomb," she says over the phone. "Like, you're really taking this and running with it."

I shrug, not that she can see me, and press the button for the seventh floor, watching the elevator doors close as Tierney prattles on in my ear.

"How'd he act when you said it?" she asks.

"I don't know. Quiet? I was sort of half asleep," I say, "but coherent enough to know what I was saying ..."

"You're so bad." She laughs. The elevator doors open and I glance out, making sure he's nowhere around before I continue this conversation. "Did he say it back?"

"Nope."

"Huh. I'd have expected him to," she says, "you know, to keep the ruse going."

"Oh, well." I dig into my purse for my keys, cradling my

phone on my shoulder, and a moment later, I'm wrapped in the chilled air of my apartment, locking the door behind me and sliding out of my shoes.

"So what's your next move?"

I grab a water from the fridge and uncap the bottle. "No idea, but I think I need to dial it down a notch. I get the feeling that the more I push, the more he pulls. Maybe I'm coming on too strong with this?"

"Do you think he knows that you know?"

"Doubt it. Marissa signed an NDA. She begged me not to tell anyone because she'd lose her job," I say. "She's not going to go from freaking out about that to running off to tell Jude she knows what he's doing."

"True." Tierney sighs. "Hey ... it's supposed to be nice the next few days and one of my friends just got back from their house in the Hamptons so it's empty ... you want to go? Get away for a little bit? They say absence makes the heart grow fonder ..."

I chuckle. "I've got him going in so many different directions right now. To go from telling him I love him to jetting off to the Hamptons for a few days is going to leave his head spinning faster than it already is."

"Good. So that's a yes?"

Taking another swig of frigid water, I mull it over, but only for a moment. "Yeah. I'm in."

"Awesome. I'll take care of our Jitney tickets and let my friend know we're using his place," she says. "I just need to clear it with my doctor and then we should be good to go. Let's plan on leaving first thing in the morning."

"Perfect."

The second I hang up the phone, the shudder of a slamming door outside in the hall grabs my attention, and I hurry toward the peephole in time to see Jude locking up and all but sprinting toward the elevator bay.

"Jude," I say, stepping out of my apartment.

He stops in his tracks, turning to face me and wearing an expression unlike any I've yet to see on his perfect face. His eyes are glassy, his smile missing, and the little indentation above his jaw pulses.

"What's going on?" I ask, closing my door and going to him.

"My niece," he says, "she was just taken by ambulance to Brooklyn Methodist. She's in the PICU now and they're trying to stabilize her."

My hand lifts to my chest. "Oh, my God."

"She had an asthma attack," he says, glancing toward the elevator. "A bad one. I have to go, I'm sorry."

"Wait," I say without giving it a second thought. He'd mentioned in the past that his sister is a single mom, and I know she has two kids. "Who's watching your other niece?"

His chest rises and falls and he's looking toward me but not at me. I've never seen Jude so distraught.

"I don't know," he manages to say, "we'll have to take turns or something."

"Let me go with you. I can help out." I don't wait for his approval before running back inside, grabbing my phone and purse and shoes, and bolting out the door.

A moment later, we're riding to the main level, dashing through the lobby, and hailing a cab outside the portico.

In this moment, I'm not worrying about what's fake or what's real. Nothing else when an innocent little girl is fighting for her life in a hospital across the city. I might be angry with him, but I'm not soulless.

We'll deal with everything later.

——

"THE END." I fold the tattered and torn waiting room book, and Ellie claps her hands.

"Again," she says, oblivious to the seriousness happening down the hall. We've been here two hours now, and I've yet to get an update from Jude, who's been consoling his sister this entire time, but I told him I'd stay here as long as they needed me to.

"Again?" I ask, tickling the sides of her ribs as she squirms against me. This will be five times now reading *Elmo's Favorite Things*, and it's not even the complete story. It appears that several pages have been ripped out, chewed on, or otherwise mangled.

Ellie nods, her dark curls falling over her big blue eyes, and she claps her hands. I turn to the first page. She's so sweet. If every baby was like this, I'd want a hundred.

I'd always wondered if I'd have been a mom by now— had things turned out differently.

A family with five small kids pours into the waiting room a few minutes later, and within seconds, the TV hanging in the corner flips to the Disney channel. A child-like cartoon princess in a purple dress steals Ellie's attention, and I quietly fold the book and place it on a nearby side table.

Ten minutes later, Ellie's body grows limp against my chest and her breathing slightly louder. When I glance down, I realize she's sleeping. With slow, careful movements, I lean down and retrieve her pink polka dot blanket from the bag I was handed along with Ellie when we got here earlier. Covering her up to stave off the waiting room chill, I rest my chin gently on the top of her head and breathe in her apple-sweet scent.

Resting my eyes for the tiniest moment, I open them a little while later to find Jude standing in the doorway, leaning against the jamb and studying us, two cups of coffee in his hands.

"Wasn't sure if you were sleeping or not there," he says as he comes toward us. Placing one of the cups next to me, he adds, "That's for you. In case you need it."

"How's she doing?" I sit up, bracing my splayed palm across Ellie's tummy so as not to wake her.

"Better," he says. "She's awake now."

"Did you know she had asthma?" I ask, "or did this come out of nowhere?"

He glances down at his coffee, pausing for a second, before his gaze lifts onto mine. "We've known for a while. I guess the inhaler Lo had on hand was empty. She couldn't find the spare and Piper was gasping for air and time was running out, so she called 9-1-1."

"I can't imagine how terrifying that must have been ... for both of them."

His teeth rake across his lower lip for a second before he takes a sip of his coffee and loses himself in thought.

"Piper's been sick ever since she was born," he says. "She was a micro preemie, so that's caused a lot of complications over the years. On top of the asthma and her partial hearing loss in one ear, she was diagnosed with juvenile diabetes earlier this year."

"I'm so sorry," I say, because no other words can do that justice.

"Lo's a great mom," he says. "She takes such good care of her girls. Today ... that was just a freak situation. Sorry I was so out of it when you saw me in the hall. I just wanted to get here as fast as I could."

"Don't apologize."

Our eyes hold and in this moment, I'm not thinking about a single thing outside these hospital walls.

"Going to go check on Lo and Piper, and then I thought I'd take Ellie home around five," he says. "She needs dinner and she needs to go to bed on time. Lo's going to stay here all night."

"I'll go with you," I say, if only because his heavy lids and baggy eyes tell me he needs all the help he can get. He looks like he just returned from the war.

"You don't have to—"

Lifting a hand, I cut him off. "I'm going with you."

———

I STAND in the middle of Lo's apartment, taking in the sights.

I think this entire place could fit into my master suite. The walls are gray-toned, the beige carpet stained and flattened, and curtains hang off the living room window from nails hammered into the trim.

A flood of toys covers the living room floor and a ménage of family photos—mostly of the girls—rest on a side table next to a pleather sofa with stuffing teeming out of the seams.

In the kitchen, an open box of store brand Cheerios sits on the counter beside an empty, overturned sippy cup.

This place is bursting with life and love and togetherness.

They might not have much, but they have each other.

"Sorry," Jude says, lifting his hand to the back of his neck when he returns from putting Ellie to bed. He studies my face, keeping his distance, like he thinks I'm seconds from trying to get the hell out of here.

I fed her chicken fingers and applesauce in the hospital cafeteria an hour ago, just before Jude came back from the PICU to get us. I thought maybe she'd have a hard time falling asleep tonight since she took that nap on me in the waiting room this afternoon, but we spent a good hour or so walking the visitor-friendly halls of the hospital, and then I took her to the park across the street to play for another hour after that.

"The place isn't usually this ... crazy," he says, moving toward the nailed curtains in the living room and inspecting them. "Huh. The others must have fallen down." He smirks. "Remind me to tell Lo she did a bang-up job fixing them."

"I'm sure she did the best she could," I say, a sleepy smile crawling across my mouth. It isn't even that late, but this day has left me zapped and lifeless.

"You're staying here, right?" he asks, detecting my exhaustion. "There's a spare room. Full-sized bed."

"I'm sleeping wherever you're sleeping tonight," I say. His mouth inches up at the sides, but only for a moment, and then it disappears altogether. For some reason, it's like he won't allow himself to be happy. Whether it has to do with his niece's situation or the fact that he feels guilty, I'll never know.

Following Jude down a small hallway, he leads me into a dark bedroom. He doesn't hit the lights, only leads me to the bed covered in messy blankets. As my eyes adjust, I make out a nightstand, a gold lamp, and a small chest of drawers in the corner.

Peeling out of my clothes, I climb beneath the cool, faux down covers and rest my head on the pillow. The bed dips on the opposite side and the covers shift a second later. Jude slides in next to me, but he doesn't pull me against him like he normally does—he keeps a safe distance.

I blame the day's events.

He doesn't have the energy to be "on," to be the Jude he's led me to believe he is.

"Thanks," he says, voice gruff and muffled as the bed shifts again. "Thanks for everything today. You didn't have to do that. Lo wanted me to tell you thanks too."

"Not a big deal at all. I'm just glad I could help. And I'm glad Piper's okay." Turning to face him, I prop myself up on my elbow. "Oh. And I didn't get a chance to tell you, but I'm going to the Hamptons with Tierney for a few days. Leaving tomorrow morning."

Jude's face winces and he lifts his hand to his face, pinching the bridge of his nose. I don't know if he's upset or relieved or if it doesn't make an ounce of a difference to him. I can't get a read on this man to save my life.

"We just planned it today," I say. "She wants one last girls' trip before the baby comes."

He's quiet, his eyes closed now as he lies on his back.

"Jude?" I ask, wanting nothing but some kind of sign that he heard me.

"Have fun, Love," he says. "I'll see you when you get back."

A moment later, he rolls away from me, burying the side of his face against a flat pillow.

Something's off.

Something's not right.

But I'll deal with it when I get back.

CHAPTER THIRTY-SIX

JUDE

LOVE CREPT out of the apartment this morning, pressing a kiss against my forehead before she dashed out the door. Her spur-of-the-moment Hamptons excursion puts a bit of a cramp in my plans, but there's nothing I can do about it. I wasn't going to tell her to stay, to keep her from having a good time with her best friend, just so I could unload this burden and break her heart.

Three days.

She'll be back in three days.

Until then ...

The soft click of the apartment lock tells me Lo's home, and I drag myself out of bed. It's still early enough that the traffic horns haven't woken Ellie, but I wasn't expecting to see Lo until later.

"Hey," I say, ambling out of my room and finger combing my messy hair into place. "Everything okay?"

Lo sits her purse on the kitchen table. "Yeah. She's ... she's doing a lot better. They think they'll send her home today. Just came home to grab a quick shower, then I'm heading back."

"I can stay with Ellie," I offer, though that goes without saying. She has no one else besides Moira Gutenberg, and she's already been gracious with her assistance this past month.

"Yeah. Thanks," Lo says, stepping out of her Chucks and kicking them aside. "Where's Love?"

"She left this morning for the Hamptons."

Lo's sunken gaze moves to mine. "The Hamptons? That's random. Didn't you two just get back from a trip?"

"Yeah." I exhale. Nothing about this past week has made sense. We had an amazing week together. She went MIA on me for a day due to a "migraine." The next day she picks up right where she left off, only this time she realizes she loves me ... and now she's taking off for three days. "I'm going to end it with her, Lo."

My sister stands by the table, hands on her hips as she searches my eyes, though for what, I'm not sure.

"Really?" she asks a moment later.

I nod.

"Wow." Lo heads to a kitchen cupboard to grab a glass before filling it with tap water. "I ... I don't know what to say. I'm proud of you for doing the right thing, but you look ... you look so ... deflated."

"The past day has been insane," I say, "and with Piper and—"

"—you love her," Lo cuts me off, hand still resting on the faucet lever.

Rolling my eyes, I say, "No. I barely knew her, Lo."

"Liar." She takes a drink of water. "But I get it. Telling yourself you don't care about her makes this easier for you."

"I'm only doing this because I *do* care about her."

Shuffling to the living room, Lo sinks into a worn seat on the edge of the sofa we bought for two hundred bucks on Craigslist last month.

"I'm sorry, Jude," Lo says, cupping the water glass in her hand as she stares ahead at a blank TV screen. "She was pretty amazing. And I know you weren't expecting that. I completely understand how that changed things for you." Pulling in a breath and letting it go, she glances back toward me. "So how are you going to do this? What are you going to say?"

Taking the lumpy chair across from her, I rest my elbows on my knees and bury my face in my hands for a second.

"I'm just going to tell her it's not working out and I'm sorry," I say, rubbing my tired eyes. "Legally ... there's nothing else I can say. Hunter had me sign that NDA. If I so much as hint about anything Hunter and I have talked about and she figures it out ... he can sue me for hundreds of thousands of dollars."

Silence lingers between us, though the whistle of water pipes in the building and the family of wild rhinos in the apartment above us fill that soundless void.

"Can't you just end it now, give her some time, and then come back into her life in a few months? People break up and get back together all the time."

Sitting back, I pick at a loose thread in the arm rest and shake my head. I've already thought about that, and it's not an option.

"If Hunter sees me back in her life a few months from now, he's going to do everything he can to destroy that," I say. "Not to mention, she'll find out I was never a 'strategic consultant.'" I drag in a haggard breath. "I'm done lying to her."

Rising from her sunken seat, Lo shuffles across the matted carpet until she's standing in front of me. We've never been a touchy-feely-huggy-affectionate family, but I get the sense that she wants to hug me right now.

"Don't," I say, placing my hand out to stop her.

Comfort and compassion are the last things I deserve.

CHAPTER THIRTY-SEVEN

LOVE

WHEN TIERNEY SAID we were staying at her friend's "beach cottage," I wasn't expecting a five-thousand-square-foot waterfront manse sitting on three acres with an unblocked view of the Atlantic.

But I managed to settle in to my private, second floor suite without a single complaint.

Sleep didn't come as easily as it should have last night despite the fact that we spent the better part of yesterday afternoon strolling the beach and walked the evening market downtown just before dinner.

I peel my eyes open and reach for my phone on my nightstand. I'd texted a little bit with Jude last night, but it was nothing more than "how are you?" and "how's Piper?" and "what are you doing?"

There was no flirting. No "I miss you." No playful banter.

Sliding out of bed, I inhale the salty breeze wafting from the cracked window in the bathroom, and I peel out of my pajamas.

Taking a good look in the mirror, I press my palms against my puffy, swollen face that hurts when I try to smile. My skin is tinged in pink along my forehead and the bridge of my nose, overly sun-kissed, and the wine and salty seafood I had last night isn't helping matters.

Still, I'm enjoying my time with Tierney, and it's kind of nice being a world away from the city and the maelstrom that has become my fake love life.

A half hour later, I'm showered for the day, donning a cornflower blue, striped cotton sundress and traipsing down the elaborate curved staircase toward the kitchen.

"Morning, sunshine," Tierney says, oddly chipper given the fact that all she did was complain about how tired she was from eight o'clock on last night.

"Thought you'd be sleeping in today." I take a seat beside her.

"Nah. Slept like a million bucks. These beds are heaven on earth." She swats her hand. "Anyway, want to walk to the market? There's this little café on the water that has the most amazing crepes you'll ever have."

Glancing out the window toward the crashing ocean waves and the smooth trail of beach where the water has washed away any remnants of our footprints, I nod.

"How's Jude?" she asks. "You hear from him?"

"We texted a little bit last night."

"How's his niece?" She begins to rise from the table, cupping her hand over her belly as she attempts to squeeze through.

"She's good. She came home." I rise, gathering my bag and phone off the counter and locating my strappy sandals and straw hat. "Is it weird that half of me doesn't want to hate him anymore?"

Tierney turns on her heel to face me, head cocked. She doesn't answer, but her silence says it all.

"I just ... it's hard to look at him and the things he does and think that he's pure evil," I say. "There's goodness in his heart. What he's doing is horrendous and indefensible, don't get me wrong, but the more I'm around him, the more I'm pretending right alongside him, the more I find myself *not* pretending. Does that make sense?"

"You've never been good at being fake." Tierney stuffs her feet into a pair of espadrille flats. "So are you saying you'd forgive him if he came clean?"

"No, not at all."

"Then what are you trying to say?"

I shrug as we head outside and Tierney locks the door behind us. "I don't know. I guess I'm trying to say that half of me can't stand him and the other half of me keeps forgetting that I can't stand him."

Tierney loops her arm over my shoulders as we head toward the path to the market.

"You want to know what I think?" she asks.

"Sure."

"Too bad. I'm not telling you." She loosens her hold on me, her arm brushing mine, and the light breeze whips her auburn hair across her smirking face. "Because it doesn't matter. All that matters is what *you* think."

"You make it sound so simple," I say, adjusting my straw hat as we walk. We take a few paces, neither of us speaking, and I lose myself in thought for a while. I don't think I can ever forgive him for lying to me, so it's pointless to entertain the fact that sometimes I forget how angry I am with him.

Grabbing my phone from my bag, I fire off an early morning text to Jude, just to keep up appearances.

"What are you doing?" I text.

"The usual," he responds a minute later.

"Consulting?" I ask.

It hit me yesterday as I was leaving his apartment in the early hours of the morning. His room was light enough that I could take a better look around, and it only took a minute for my blurry gaze to hone in on the guitars resting in stands in the corner, the closet door half open and offering a glimpse of men's clothes hanging on plastic hangers, and on my way out, I passed a stack of mail sitting on the kitchen table, the bill on top addressed to Jude Warner and the address matching the apartment.

We didn't sleep in his sister's guest room that evening—that was his room. His *real* room.

And he's not a "strategic consultant." I imagine Hunter dreamed up that phony title for him to go with his phony wardrobe and his phony apartment.

"Not today," he responds a second later.

It might be the truest thing he's ever said to me.

CHAPTER THIRTY-EIGHT

JUDE

"THE FUCK." I nearly choke on my words when I return from my run and find Hunter LeGrand standing in the middle of the apartment.

"Two million," he says, arms folded across his narrow chest.

"What? *No.*" My jaw clenches and the pulse point in my neck throbs. The sight of this douchebag's unexpected presence sends my blood pressure soaring. "What are you doing here?"

"Giving you one last chance to finish what you started."

"You're wasting your time."

"Have you ended it already?" he asks.

"Tomorrow," I say.

His lips crack into a smile that has no business being on his smug face because I'm not changing my mind.

"All right then." His hands press together. "One last time ... two million dollars."

Heading to the door, I yank it open and nod for him to leave. If he's lucky, I might let him leave without telling him exactly what I think of him—not that he'd care, and he probably already knows what he is. But a not-so-gentle reminder couldn't hurt.

"Fine," he says, feet planted. "Five million."

"You might as well be talking about Monopoly money, Hunter, because it's just paper to me."

His self-righteous smile fades and his complexion darkens.

"What's this about anyway? Why do you want someone to marry her?" I ask. He wouldn't tell me before due to "liability reasons," but now that the deal's off, it shouldn't matter. "And why the hell is it worth millions of dollars to you?"

Hunter releases an incredulous laugh. "You don't get it at all, and I suppose you wouldn't ... alimony."

"Alimony? What about it?"

"Once she's married and becomes someone else's problem, I no longer have to donate millions of my hard-earned dollars to a woman who didn't do a damn thing to earn them. That manhating judge let her make off like a bandit, and then she gave her alimony on top of it. Can you believe that shit? What gives her the right to give away my money like that?"

Raking my hand across my jaw, I have to look away for a second to keep myself from knocking him to the floor.

"So Love didn't stand by you and support you while you made your first million?" I ask. "She didn't put her dreams on hold so you could chase yours?"

"I don't see how that's any of your business," he says.

"And honestly, let's be real. You were nothing but hired help. The details of this arrangement have nothing to do with you and quite frankly, you have no right to concern yourself with them."

Hired help.

I suppose he's right. But it doesn't change the fact that he's the biggest piece of shit I've ever met in my life—right up there with my father. Only difference between them are a few metal bars and the disproportionate size of their bank accounts.

"Five million," Hunter says, finally strutting toward the door. "Take it or leave it."

The tautness in my jaw sends a dull ache radiating up the sides of my face, threatening the beginnings of a tension headache.

"Fuck off, Hunter."

He stops in his tracks, turning on his Prada loafers and charging toward me until his face is way too fucking close to mine.

"Your key," he says, holding out his hand. "Give me your apartment key."

Releasing a forced breath, I grip the metal of the key until I feel the indentations in my palm.

"The *key*, Jude," he says, harder this time. "Take any personal belongings and leave everything else. Including the phone. I'll be sure to let the doorman know you're not to set foot in this building again."

I don't have Love's number memorized—it was only ever programmed into the phone he gave me. And if I'm banned from the building, I won't be able to come back and talk to her in person.

She'll come home from her trip and I'll be gone and that will be that.

Slapping the key on the counter, I lock eyes with the revolting excuse for a man standing in front of me.

"You're pathetic," I tell him before leaving to grab my guitar—the only thing that truly belongs to me in this apartment.

Everything else was a prop, part of a costume I agreed to wear when I made a deal with the devil himself.

Hunter smirks, like he finds my insult funny.

"I don't feel bad for you," he says as I head out. "You knew what you signed up for, and you fell for her anyway."

How could I *not*?

Being with her was so effortless, so natural.

I never expected to hit it off with her.

And I never expected her to be everything Hunter said she wasn't.

Stopping in the doorway, my fist clenches at my side, and I start to say something but stop myself. He's not worthy of the oxygen it would take to tell him exactly what I think of him one last time.

Turning to leave, I clutch the strap of my guitar case and slam the door behind me. Pausing in front of Love's door, I wish she were standing right here so I could tell her how sorry I am.

And how much I love her.

CHAPTER THIRTY-NINE

LOVE

"SO WEIRD," I mumble, checking my Messages app for the hundredth time today.

"What?" Tierney moves her hat out of her eyes and squints toward me.

"I've been texting Jude all day and the messages aren't even showing as read." I flip the screen of my phone to show her. "First one was sent at eight fifteen this morning. I sent four others throughout the day. It's been almost eleven hours. This isn't normal."

The dusky sky and crashing of the ocean against rocks paints the prettiest backdrop to our last sunset in the Hamptons, but I can't appreciate any of it because despite the fact I have no business caring about this nonsense, I'm desperate to figure out what the hell is going on with him.

He was hired to make me fall in love with him, and just

when I've led him to believe he's on the right path ... he pulls away.

"Maybe he changed read receipt settings?" she asks.

"Why would he do that *now*?"

"Why does it bother you so much?" she asks, reaching for her virgin margarita. "Because it shouldn't. You two aren't really together. You're both pretending."

"I know." I exhale, wishing I didn't care, wishing it didn't bother me, wishing I knew if he knows that *I* know.

"Why don't you go inside and top off your wine," Tierney says, "and when you come back out here, we can pretend the jackass no longer exists."

Glancing at my empty wine glass, I peel myself out of the teak lounger, tie my sarong around my waist, and head inside for a refill, only to find the bottle empty. Heading to the wine cellar down the hall, I locate another bottle of Riesling and hunt down the wine opener. By the time I'm finished and my glass is more than half full, I make my way back to the beach.

"Love, I made us some new friends!" Tierney flags me down as I make my way down the stone steps of the patio, toward the cabana we set up on the sand earlier today.

Two masculine forms fill the space beside Tierney's chair, though I can only see them from the shoulders down ... until I get closer.

"Oh, my god, Tierney ... " I fight a smirk and mumble under my breath as soon as their faces come into focus, and once I arrive at our spot, it takes all the strength I have not to ogle and gawk in a way that makes it painfully obvious.

They're gorgeous.

Tanned, rippled abs.

Thick heads of chocolate hair, both varying degrees of sun-kissed.

Full lips.

Strong jaws.

Big *hands* ...

"Love, this is Dmitri," she says, pointing to the man in the yellow board shorts who lifts the beer in his hand and nods. "And this is his brother, Sascha. Guys, this is my best friend, Love. And yes, that's her real name."

Sascha is taller than Dmitri by an inch or two, his shoulders broader and his hair a shade darker. His clear blue eyes are fixed on me, lit almost.

"They're staying two doors down," she adds. "They just got here today. Told them we're leaving tomorrow, but they can hang out with us tonight if they want."

Sometimes I swear she forgets she's married and pregnant.

"Nice to meet you," I move my wine to my left hand and offer my right. Dmitri laughs but Sascha comes to my rescue, letting his handshake linger a few beats longer than necessary.

"They're business partners," Tierney says. "What do you guys do again?"

"We work in renewable energy," Sascha says, looking directly at me. There's a hint of an exotic accent in his voice, Eastern European, perhaps. And he speaks with careful intention, the syllables rolling off his tongue. "What is it you do, Love?"

"I'm in the process of opening a women's center in Brooklyn," I say, taking a seat in my lounger.

His eyes track my every move and his full mouth curls at one side. "That's incredible. What made you want to do that?"

He asks all the questions I don't feel like answering, but

I answer them as best I can anyway in the name of honesty because there isn't enough of it in this world.

I got divorced ...

I came into some money ...

I wanted to do something good with it ...

Sascha doesn't bat an eye, instead he keeps the conversation moving full steam ahead, asking where I'm from, where I went to college, and what I do for fun on the weekends.

Every so often I glance at Tierney, who throws me a wink or some side eye with a side of a smile that reeks of "he's so fucking into you right now!"

Sascha is beautiful in a way that most men aren't. A skilled conversationalist. An enthusiastic listener. Infinitely curious. And there's a gentle, unguarded demeanor about him.

But when I look at him, I feel nothing in all the places I should at least be feeling *something.*

There are no butterflies, no thrumming heart, no head rush.

Dmitri's phone lights in his hand, and he lifts the screen to his face. A second later, he nudges Sascha.

"Hey, we're going to meet up with some of our friends downtown," Sascha says. "You guys want to join us?"

Tierney lifts her palms. "Think I'm going to keep my eight months pregnant ass here, but thanks for the invite. Love, you should go though. If you want."

I shoot her a look, eyes hardening. A silent, sarcastic thank you for putting me on the spot.

"We're leaving tomorrow, so I don't want to stay out late," I say, turning to Sascha. "Otherwise I'd join you."

His crystalline gaze steadies onto mine. "That's too bad."

Dmitri lifts his brows, waiting as his brother stands there with his feet cemented to the sand.

"Hey, I'm going to be in the city after this for the next few months for work," he says. "Mind if I look you up when I get there?"

I don't have to look at Tierney to feel the mile-wide smile radiating off her face.

"Yeah, no, that'd be great," I say, though I don't one hundred percent believe myself.

Sascha dips his hand into the pocket of his striped board shorts and retrieves his phone before handing it to me, and I'm instantly taken back to the day Jude asked for my phone so he could program his number into my contacts.

I offer a gracious smile and add my number to his phone under "Love (real name) Aldridge," and when I hand it back, he chuckles through his nose.

"Cute," he says, gaze lifting back to mine like a gentle ocean breeze. "I'll definitely call you."

With that, he gives a quick wave, tells Tierney it was nice to meet her, and follows his brother up the beach.

"Oh, my god, Love." Tierney leans toward me, her manicured fingers digging into my arm. "That was random."

"Yeah." I grab my wine and take a sip, watching Sascha's strapping figure grow smaller in the distance.

"He's *sooooo* into you." Tierney rubs her hands together like the crazy person that she currently is.

"Okay." I shrug, taking another sip.

"Oh, stop. Don't act coy. He's probably one of the hottest guys I've ever seen in the Hamptons in my life, and he couldn't take his eyes off you for two seconds."

"Whatever. He was just being nice."

"Nice, my pregnant ass." She rolls her eyes. "If he calls you and asks you on a date, are you going to go?"

"If he even calls me."

"He will," she says. "And when he does ... you're going to say yes. Right?"

Pulling in a breath of salty, oceanic air, I respond with a simple, "We'll see."

Heading in for the night a little while later, I trek upstairs and get ready for bed, realizing that I haven't so much as thought about Sascha since he left.

The attention was flattering.

The conversation was enjoyable.

Asking for my number was a charming move.

But at the end of the night, Sascha is the least of my concerns because I still can't stop wondering why Jude hasn't read a single text of mine today.

CHAPTER FORTY

JUDE

THEY SAY if you rip a Band-Aid off quickly, it hurts less.

I don't know about that.

I've spent the last twenty-four hours feeling the sting of that rip, but I know it'll be nothing compared to what Love's about to go through.

Any minute now, she's going to come back to The Jasper, knock on my door, and eventually realize I'm not there anymore. Maybe the super will tell her I moved out. Maybe Raymond will tell her I've been blacklisted. That combined with the fact that she has no way to reach me is going to make her think I ghosted her, and knowing her, she's going to blame herself. She's going to think it's because she told me she loved me.

And that's how it looks.

She told me she loved me and I bolted.

Her love will eventually be displaced by revulsion, but that's the way it was going to go down in the end anyway.

Strolling down Neptune Avenue, I stop next to a couple at a crosswalk and wait for the light. From the corner of my eye, I see them nuzzling, laughing, clasping hands and slowly bumping into each other, like they can't go more than two point four seconds without touching in some capacity.

Wasn't long ago, I knew that feeling.

The yellow-haired girl rises on her toes and kisses her boyfriend—the way Love always had to rise on her toes to kiss me—and my knotted stomach sinks.

The crosswalk lights and I get ahead of them because I can't take another second of watching some of the happiest moments of my life play out in front of me in real time.

A block or so ahead, I see a "Coming Soon" sign in a storefront window, and once I'm closer, I realize it's the building we toured for Agenda W.

Everything happened so fast, and it ended just as quickly.

I blinked and I met her.

I blinked and I lost her.

I lived for those moments in between.

My only wish now is that someday I might run into her, might get a chance to tell her that I'm sorry—even if she doesn't believe me and even if it doesn't matter. I just want her to hear those words from the very lips that had no right kissing her in the first place.

Keeping my stride, I make my way to the pharmacy on the corner to grab Piper's insulin. An older man in a Mets t-shirt waits before me, but other than that, the place is unusually slow for this time of day.

I slide my hand in my back pocket to grab my phone, but there's nothing there.

I must have left it at home.

"Next," a woman's voice calls a moment later as the man in front of me shuffles away with a white paper bag in hand.

"Here to pick up for Piper Cunningham," I say, grabbing my wallet.

The pharmacy tech working the register gives a warm smile, her eyes gliding back and forth between her computer screen and me.

"Whoops," she says, waving her hand in the air. "I typed the wrong name. What did you say your name was again?"

"It's for Piper Cunningham," I say, enunciating every damn syllable because I don't have all day. Lo has to head to work soon and I've got to pick up a pizza for us on the way home.

"No, what's your name?" she says, flashing her oversized smile. "For the notes."

"Jude," I say. "Jude Warner."

"Thank you, Jude Warner." She says my full name, and I think of Love. But then again, I'm always thinking of Love. "Okay, let me grab that for you. Two seconds ..."

She trots off to the back and returns thirty seconds later with a white bag.

"Okay, with insurance, today's total is going to be three-hundred six dollars and eleven cents," she says.

I don't bat an eye as I grab my card. Hunter had given me an advance, most of which I used to pay our rent for the next six months, and I'd also set aside several grand for Piper's medicine. He hasn't asked for any of it back, and I don't think he ever will because fifty grand is probably pocket change to him.

"You look really familiar," the girl says, pointing her

finger and squinting as I sign for the meds. "Have we met before? Do I know you somehow?"

I've never seen this girl before in my life. If I had to guess, I'd say she's all of twenty-two. I've got damn near an entire decade on her. I highly doubt our paths have ever crossed.

"I don't think so," I say, eyes lifting to her name tag, "Britney."

Her thin lips bunch at one side. "I don't know ... "

If this is her lame attempt at flirting with me or feeling me out, she's wasting her time.

I slide my debit card and punch in the PIN.

"Receipt?" she asks.

"No thanks." I tuck the bag under my arm and get the hell out of there before she has a chance to stall me with that nonsense again.

━━━

"YOU'RE BACK!" Lo rushes up to the door the second I walk into the apartment, her hands clapping as she does a little dance. "Thank god."

"What?"

"You left your phone here."

"I know. I forgot it." I push past her, placing the meds on the kitchen table. "Sorry."

"No, you missed a call," she says, grabbing my arm and turning me around.

My heart climbs up my throat and my mouth runs dry.

Love.

"Jude, your old boss called," Lo continues. "He said they just landed a huge contract and they're hiring back all the guys they laid off ... he wants you to come back as soon as possible! Isn't that great?"

My sister does a little dance before flinging her arms around my shoulders.

"Yeah," I say. "Best news I've had in a while."

CHAPTER FORTY-ONE

LOVE

I'M BEGINNING to get used to waking up in a cold bed, alone. I don't even search for his warmth anymore. Kicking the covers off, I slide out of bed and trudge to the bathroom to wash up before trudging to the kitchen to make some plain oatmeal. After three days in the Hamptons filled with buttery seafood and an endless supply of fine wines, I need to give my body a break.

Grabbing a packet from the cupboard, I rip the paper and dump the contents into a bowl before topping it off with water and sliding it into the microwave. There's something about the hum of a microwave that puts me in a trance-like state, helps me to zone out. Only this time, my peaceful hum is interrupted by the sound of men's voices and the clink of metal.

The first thing I did when I got home last night was text Jude to let him know I was back. My message, like all the others before it, went unread. As soon as I got myself settled and changed, I headed across the hallway to his door, knocking a handful of times, but his apartment was eerily quiet.

No footsteps. No voices. No soft hum of a baseball game on the TV.

Needless to say, no one was home.

That or he was sleeping?

Following the sounds, I dash toward my door and peer through the peephole.

Jude's door is open.

A second later, a man stands in the doorway, motioning at someone down the hall. A second later, another man appears with a metal dolly. Sprinting down the hall, I grab my robe off the hook in the master bathroom and cover my pajamas before rushing out the door.

"Excuse me," I say to a bald man with a hooked nose and clipboard. "What's going on here?"

"And you are?" He glances at his clipboard before looking back at me.

"I'm a friend of the tenant's," I say.

"Okay, so if you two are friends, then you know he moved." The man steps away from me, yelling at one of the guys coming off the elevator. "Down here, Marius!"

I try to respond but the words are trapped, stuck in my throat as I struggle to breathe. My stomach caves, same as if I'd been knifed, and my palms soothe an imaginary wound.

"I knew he'd be moving," I finally manage to say. "Just didn't think it would be this soon. Thank you for your time." Turning, I duck back into my apartment.

So much for vindication.

So much for closure of any sort.

These last several days, I've suffered through mixed

feelings ... asking myself if I truly hate him or if I'm capable of forgiving him for what he's done because I convinced myself that he's a good person underneath it all.

But I was wrong because good people don't do this. They don't just disappear out of your life without warning.

He screwed me every which way he could—literally, emotionally, and almost figuratively—and I don't even get a *goodbye?*

Locating my phone in my room, I fire off a text to Jude's number. I don't expect him to read it since he hasn't read any of the others, but I need to get a few things off my chest.

"Wow, Jude," I write, "Way to sweep me off my feet and then leave without so much as a goodbye. I thought I knew you. Turns out I had you all wrong. You're a selfish coward and I'll forever regret the day we met."

I press send and watch the screen for a few moments, only a little red exclamation point pops up beside my message. I press the icon to try to send it again, but it fails to go through. After a few more failed attempts, I dial his damn number so I can say these things to his face—or let's be real here, probably his voicemail.

"We're sorry. The number you have dialed has been disconnected ..."

Ending the call, I sink back into my bed pillows and draw my legs against my chest. Of course he disconnected his number. Why wouldn't he? He completely removed himself from every aspect of my life.

I call Tierney.

"He's gone," I say when she answers.

"Who?"

"Jude. Who else?" I ask.

She groans. "I thought we were pretending he no longer existed?"

"Guess we don't have to pretend anymore. His place is being packed up and his phone is disconnected."

"He ghosted you."

"He ghosted me," I echo, but only because "ghosted" sounds more indifferent than "abandoned," and I'm not quite ready to admit that I let my feelings get away from me.

I feel for him.

I freaking fell for him.

Letting that thought sink in for a moment, I find my breath shallowing and my skin abuzz with the kind of out-of-control anxiousness I've only known twice in my life before: first when Dad passed and then again when proof of Hunter's infidelity plastered my phone screen.

Tierney clears her throat. "I can hire someone to find him if you want. I think Josh knows a guy."

"Nah. I'm pretty sure he's back in Brooklyn." I shake this off. I have to. I can't wallow in the dissolution of something that never should've happened in the first place. Exhaling, I pick at a loose thread in my comforter before getting the urge to burn the stupid thing. "But it doesn't matter. It's done. It's over. Just wish I would've confronted him when I had the chance instead of carrying on like some lovesick stage five clinger."

"You were just keeping your word to Marissa. You promised you wouldn't say anything."

"I know." I pull in a deep breath. "I really wanted to call him out. I wanted to look him in the eye and ask him why."

"Go to Brooklyn and ask him."

I chuff. "He's not worth the cab fare."

"Hey, Love, I've got a conference call in two minutes. Call you back later?" she asks.

"Of course."

I pull the phone away from my ear and watch the

screen go dark when she hangs up, but before I place it back on the charger, I pull up my photos. Scrolling past the recent ones from my getaway with Tierney, I find a whole myriad of photos Jude and I had taken together—mostly selfies—and I study our faces, our smiles, the positions of our hands, all the things that probably don't matter at this point, but still, a part of me wants to know if any of it was ever real for him.

Swiping a few more times, I stop when I come across a photo of me that he took when I wasn't looking. I'm sitting at a little wrought iron table outside a coffee shop, reading a book I'd picked up that morning. There's a wildflower—one he'd picked for me on the way—tucked behind one ear, and I'm completely engrossed in my tome.

I swipe again. And again. Stopping when I find another photo he took of me when I wasn't looking. This one's from the week of Cameo's wedding. I'm dancing with my grandmother at the reception—*Jump, Jive and Wail* I think it was, and he snapped the photo mid-twirl.

By the time I finish going through the rest of the photos, I find a handful of other candid shots, all of them almost artistic in nature, framed and angled perfectly, capturing the beauty in all of these mundane little moments.

Why would he do that if this entire thing was nothing but a meaningless charade?

CHAPTER FORTY-TWO

JUDE

"VINNIE, hand me that basin wrench, will you?" I ask, crouched beneath the sink in a remodeled hospital bathroom.

It's been a week since I left The Jasper, guitar in hand.

I keep expecting to get a knock at the door. I keep waiting for her to come and find me, to demand to know why I walked out of her life ... but the knock never comes.

Today marks four days back with Premier Plumb and Supply.

It also marks four days working at Lenox Hill Hospital on the Upper East Side—Love's stomping grounds.

Every morning when I get here, I search the sidewalks for her face. When I leave for lunch, I do the same. The end of the day is no different. I don't even know what I'd do if I ran into her ... guess I just want to see if she's okay.

"Hey, Vinnie," I say, turning the wrench. "What's the worst thing you've ever done before?"

Vinnie lets out a big-bellied chuckle. "Can you get more specific? I've done a lot of shit in my day, kid."

He always calls me "kid" despite the fact that I'm thirty and he's only got about twelve years on me, if that.

"What's the worst thing you've ever done to a woman," I say, "like a girlfriend or your wife or something."

Crouching down and grabbing a strap wrench from the box between us, he groans as he rises, his knees popping.

"I dunno, kid," he says. "I did a lot of shit in my younger days, but I've been married thirteen years now and never once cheated on my old lady, so I like to think that makes up for it. Why do you ask? You do something? You having lady troubles?"

I sniff. "Something like that."

"Lay it on me. Maybe I can help."

"It's a long story. Complicated." I twist the wrench again and check the fitting to make sure it's secure before climbing out from under there.

"Kid, the day is young. It's you and me for the next eight hours."

"I can't tell if you're being nosy or if you genuinely want to be helpful."

Vinnie chuckles. "Little of both, maybe. If I'm being honest."

"This guy basically hired me to date his ex." I can't give him specifics due to the NDA, but I can give him the gist of the situation.

"Ooooh," Vinnie claps his hands together. "I knew it was going to be good, but I didn't know it was going to be this good. She find out?"

"Nah," I say. "I ended up liking her. She ended up

liking me. I was going to break it off because it was the right thing to do, only I never got the chance. Her ex basically removed me from the situation."

"Damn."

"She thinks I left without saying goodbye." I dig around in the tool box until I find the connector o-ring I'm looking for. "Just hate that I hurt her, and I hate that I never got to say sorry."

"Listen." Vinnie splays his hand flat and leans close, like he's about to give me some advice under the table. "Women are the weaker sex—but only physically. Their hearts are Teflon. I swear to you. They can take a hit emotionally and you'd never be able to tell. Resilient, that's what they are. Anyway, I assure you, she's going to move on and she's going to forget all about you. You'll just be that jerk ex that she's always afraid she's going to run into. Don't beat yourself up about the way it went down."

We finish up this bathroom before starting on the next and by the time we're finished with that one, it's lunch.

"You want anything from the deli?" I offer Vinnie before dodging out.

"Nah. I'm hitting up the cafeteria today."

I check the time and head toward the deli up the street from The Jasper. Love and I used to stop there sometimes, and every once in a while she'd pop in there for blueberry bagels and coffee.

Every day this week I've grabbed lunch from there. I suppose it's because it's the only place I can go where I still *feel* her. And sometimes, I swear I see the two of us standing in line, my hands around her waist. She's smiling, resting the back of her head against my shoulder as she studies the menu even though she gets the same thing every time.

But today, just like the last few days, I hit the deli, stand in line, order my lunch, and leave without a single sign of Love.

On the way back to Lenox Hill, I take a detour past The Jasper and kill the extra fifteen minutes I have left, stopping at the fountain.

Two kids splash in the water, dipping their hands over the marble ledge and laughing, and two teenage girls take a selfie in front of the sculpture of the couple under the umbrella. I sit for a moment, taking it all in. The sights. The sounds. The reminders of some of the happiest weeks I've ever known.

And when it's time to leave, I pass the fountain one last time, tossing in a quarter for no reason at all.

CHAPTER FORTY-THREE

LOVE

WITH AN ARMFUL OF GROCERY BAGS, I maneuver the Fifth Avenue sidewalks, making a beeline for my building the second I spot it. By the time I reach the lobby, my arms are dying. I thought about having my groceries delivered, but I needed to get out of the apartment today. I needed to do something normal and ordinary and productive.

Passing under the black awning and heading toward the lobby, I glance toward the fountain for a split second. And in that split second, I spot a man with Jude's sandy hair and tall swagger, but it's only the back of him.

From here I make out a stained white t-shirt and ragged jeans, and then he's gone.

I doubt it was him, but only because I see him everywhere. I see him in places he couldn't possibly be. It isn't fair the way my mind constantly plays tricks on me when all I want to do is forget he was ever a part of my life.

Sometimes I think about what I'd say to him if I ever run into him, and I always decide I'd ask one question and one question only: why?

Nothing else matters.

Heading inside, I make my way to my apartment and unload my groceries with shaky arms that tell me I need to incorporate push-ups into my daily routine.

The buzz of my phone in my purse fills my quiet apartment as I place the last item in a cupboard, and when I retrieve it, Tierney's name flashes on the screen.

"Hey," I answer, cradling the phone on my shoulder as I reach for a stack of mail I've yet to sort. "What's up?"

"Love, it's Josh." Tierney's husband is on the other end, his voice breathy and his words hurried. "Tierney's in labor and we're en route to Lenox Hill, but we don't have time to stop at home and grab her overnight bag."

She wasn't due for two more weeks ... I bet she's freaking the hell out right now.

"I'm on it," I say. Tierney's voice is muffled in the background, but I can hear her rhythmic panting followed by the distinct sound of a woman in severe pain. My uterus cringes in sympathy. "I'll be there as soon as I can."

Ordering an Uber, I collect my keys and wallet and book it to the lobby to wait for my ride. Tierney lives in the Upper West Side, so we zag across the city before zipping back to 77th where the driver deposits me at the main entrance of the hospital also known as "The Lenox Hilton." At least that's what Tierney told me after she toured birthing suites that came complete with private chefs.

I locate the maternity ward and drop her bag off at the front desk, texting Tierney and Josh's phones to know it's there, and then I find a spot in the waiting room and grab a *Better Homes and Gardens* magazine from a stack on the table beside me. It was either that, *Hi-Lites,* or *Country Living.*

I'm halfway finished with an article on how to roast rutabagas the proper way when Josh bursts through the waiting room doors in scrubs, a delirious smile on his face. Scanning the waiting room, he finally finds me.

"It's a boy!" he says.

"Holy shit, she had the baby already?" I rise from my chair, feeling as dazed as Josh looks. Though I shouldn't be surprised, Tierney's as impatient as they come. It's only fitting that her firstborn child is too.

Josh makes his way toward me and I give him a congratulatory hug. He hasn't stopped beaming since he burst through those doors.

"We thought she was going to be delivering in the lobby. Barely made it up here in time," he says with a soft chuckle, though I can only imagine how terrified he was at the time. "They're still cleaning him up, but I'll come back and get you in a few so you can meet him."

"Can't wait."

———

"THIS IS FOR SURE YOUR KID," I say. Holden Joshua Castle is the spitting image of his mother. "Dramatic entrance. Full head of auburn hair. Loud voice. Loves to sleep."

Tierney watches as I cradle her baby in my arms and sway back and forth, soaking in his sweet perfection. Baby Holden rests in my arms, sleeping with his little hands tucked against his face, not a care in the world. He's completely in the moment, as he should be. He doesn't care where he came from. He's not worried about where he's going (yet). He's just here. With us.

Studying his button nose and rosy lips and chubby cheeks, I see more than a newborn baby. I see a new beginning. I decide right here, right now that as soon as I leave this room, I'm only focusing on the things that matter, things that make my life better.

Nothing else is worthy of my time or energy.

I promise to live in the moment and embrace it.

I promise to be present so I can experience life in real time and not in flashback reels in my mind as I lie in bed at night thinking of all the ways I could've handled things differently.

"Love?" Tierney asks.

I glance up from Holden. "Yeah?"

"Can I have my baby back?"

Chuckling, I carry him back to the hospital bed, back to Tierney's warm embrace, teary eyes, and swollen face.

"What kind of parents do you think you'll be?" I ask when Josh comes back from making calls.

Tierney shrugs, her gaze still glued to her baby like she can't believe he's real. "The kind that wing it?"

"We didn't read a single baby book," Josh says. "Didn't take a single class."

"Am I supposed to be impressed by that or concerned for the welfare of the child?" I tease. The two of them are the most laidback couple I've ever met. They won't be helicopter parents who pawn their child off on nannies and keep their child psychiatrist on speed dial in case of. "I kid. Holden's a lucky little guy. He's going to have a blast with you guys."

A knock at the door steals our moment, and a second

later, Tierney's parents shuffle in, arms full of flowers and balloons. Heartfelt sentiments fill the room. Camera flashes. Oohs and aahs every time Holden yawns or makes a face as he soils his tiny diaper.

Rising on my toes, I mouth to Tierney that I'm going to run and grab a bite to eat.

Sneaking out of the room, I follow the signs to the cafeteria, which of course is in an entirely different wing and several floors below and this hospital is basically a maze, but I continue on my quest.

Turning a corner at the end of a long hall, I stop short, nearly tripping myself, to avoid colliding with a man in a white t-shirt.

"I'm so sor—" I'm silenced when I find myself staring at a familiar pair of dusty green eyes, only the rest of him is unrecognizable. His hair is messy, slightly longer than before, and it's matted against his forehead like he's kept it under a hat most of the day. His jeans, stained and torn, hang low on his hips, and a tool belt is secured around his narrow waist. "Jude?"

CHAPTER FORTY-FOUR

JUDE

"LOVE." I say the name I never thought I'd get a chance to say out loud again. I always thought seeing her again would be surreal or dreamlike, but this is anything but. She's standing so close I can smell her faded perfume and her favorite lavender conditioner. I can hear her breaths as they shorten and quicken the longer she stares at me. I could reach out and touch her if I wanted to—but I won't. "What are you doing here? Are you okay?"

The shock on her face fades, replaced with a line between her brows.

Taking a step back, she says, "You don't get to ask me that."

"Love," I begin to say, but she bypasses me and continues down the hall. Following after her, I catch up with her next to a service elevator.

She looks amazing: her blonde hair dripping in soft

waves around her face, her lips slicked in cherry Chapstick, nothing but Levi's and a t-shirt to complete her look.

"How much do you know?" I ask, knowing full well this is dangerous territory. I'm not allowed to bring any of this up to her, let alone speak to her.

Her arms fold across her chest. She won't look at me. "I know enough."

Releasing a harbored breath, I say the words I never thought I'd get a chance to say, "I'm so sorry, Love."

Her glassy hazel eyes flick to mine for a second before returning to the carpeted floor.

"There's so much I wish I could tell you ... but I can't," I say. "And I can't even tell you why I can't tell you." I huff. "But I want you to know, that the parts that mattered? The parts where you felt something? That was real. I felt something too."

She says nothing, only stands there with her arms tight against her chest, worrying her bottom lip.

"I miss you," I say. "I think about you every single day."

I leave it at that because I've already said too much, and it seems to be falling on deaf ears anyway.

We stand in silence for a minute, still and unmoving. I'm not going anywhere unless she wants me to.

A moment later, Love finally looks at me again, her full lips parting as she begins to say something.

"Goodbye, Jude." Pushing past me, she heads back toward the hallway where we collided and I stay put until she disappears.

I thought I'd feel better once I got the chance to see her again and finally apologize. Turns out I was wrong. Seeing Love so guarded, so closed off, so different from the woman I got to know, only adds to my guilt. And knowing she was right in front of me and I couldn't touch her, couldn't kiss her, sends a tightness to my chest that threatens to steal the air from my lungs.

I can only hope she heard what she needed to hear tonight and that it's all she needs to move on and find someone who can make her as happy as she made me.

That's all I want for her.

CHAPTER FORTY-FIVE

LOVE

"WHO'S NEXT?" Cameo scans the sheet of paper I gave her this morning when we first arrived at my newly-leased Agenda W building for interviews.

By the time her honeymoon tan faded, Cameo realized that being a stay at home housewife isn't as glamourous as she thought it would be and promptly booked a flight to the city to help me staff this place. Plus, she thinks I'm falling apart ever since the Jude thing came to light and she said she feels like she needs to be here to get me through this.

But I'm not complaining. Help is help.

"Connie Berger," I say, reading off the list. "But that's not until one."

It's been a week since I ran into Jude at Lenox Hill Hospital, and now that Agenda W is getting off the ground, I'm going to be spending a lot more time in Brooklyn. I'm bound to run into him again, and every time I step outside this building, I find myself scanning the area, wondering if he's in the vicinity.

I wanted to tell him off last week. And I was so close. But something stopped me, something held me back. Every time I tried, I couldn't get the words off my tongue.

Maybe it was softness in his eyes, the remorse in his tone, or the apology I wasn't expecting ... but I found myself speechless.

And then I got the hell out of there.

"Think I'm going to grab some fresh air and an iced coffee. Want anything?" I ask Cameo as she thumbs through honeymoon pictures on her phone and posts one on her Instagram with a "throwback Thursday" hashtag.

"No, thank you." She grabs her Dean and Deluca cup lifting it to show me.

Only the best for Cam.

Slipping my bag over my shoulder, I head out and walk two blocks to a Starbucks on the corner. It's late July and literally hot as hell, but the sun feels nice as it warms the top of my head, and the cold coffee is going to be just what I need to get through the rest of the interviews this afternoon.

Heading in once I get there, I find a place in line and peruse the menu even though I already know what I'm getting.

"Love?"

I follow the voice coming from my left until my gaze lands on a raven-haired beauty navigating a double stroller through a sea of tables-for-two.

"Lo," I say, heart ricocheting as I glance around to ensure it's just her and the girls. "Hi."

"How've you been?" she asks.

It's strange that she would ask me that, given the fact that we only met a couple of times and only for the briefest of moments, but she looks at me like she knows me inside and out and the tenderness in her voice suggests her question is genuine.

"Great," I say, inching forward as the line moves "You?"

Her eyes search mine, though for what, I'm not sure.

"We're doing well," she says, biting the corner of her lip.

The line moves again, but Lo is caught behind a display on the other side and a small table prevents her from wedging her way closer.

"He fell in love with you," she blurts.

"What?" Michael Bublé croons over the speakers, and I'm not sure I heard her right.

"He fell in love with you," she repeats, this time a little louder. A woman reading on her tablet glances over at us before returning to her book. "I think he still loves you. And I think a part of him always will ... for what it's worth."

"Excuse me, sorry." I push my way toward the end of the line, not wanting to have this conversation in this manner, and when I finally reach her, I ask, "If he loved me, why'd he just ... leave? Without saying a single word?"

Lo begins to say something and then stops, her shoulders falling. "That's how it had to be, and that's all I can say."

"All right." I turn back toward the line, taking a new spot at the very back.

"That guy ... your ex ... he made Jude sign an NDA," she says. "He can't tell you anything or he'll get sued. Believe me, Love, he wanted to explain. He wanted to tell you everything."

Of course.

"I know I'm his sister and I'm biased, but believe me when I say sometimes good people make bad choices. He made a mistake, Love. A huge mistake. A selfish mistake—

honestly the first selfish mistake the man's ever made in his life." Lo lifts her hand to her heart, brows lifting beneath her dark bangs. "It cost him dearly, and he still hasn't forgiven himself. I don't think he ever will."

If she's trying to make me reconsider my stance on forgiving him ... it's working. But only a little. And I keep that to myself.

Ellie begins to squirm in her half of the stroller and Piper tugs at the hem of Lo's shirt.

"Anyway, I just wanted to tell you he loved you. That's all," she says before pushing her stroller toward the door. A hipster in a beanie holds the door for them as she squeezes through, and a second later they're gone.

I can't deny how validating it feels to hear those words, but it doesn't change what he did.

Or the devastating profoundness of his betrayal.

CHAPTER FORTY-SIX

JUDE

"GUESS WHO I RAN INTO TODAY?" Lo asks when I get home from work.

"Who?" I slide my shoes off and sort through a stack of mail, mostly bills.

"Love."

Glancing up from the power bill in my hand, I'm surprised to find a wild-eyed grin on my sister's face, like she's harboring good news. But I don't want to get my hopes up. Last week when I ran into Love at the hospital, it didn't exactly go that well.

"She was getting coffee," Lo says. "Anyway, I talked to her for a few minutes."

"And?" I wind my hand, willing her to get on with her story.

"I told her that you still love her and you haven't forgiven yourself," she says.

Exhaling, I return to the mail in my hands. I said something similar last week and didn't get anywhere with her.

"Why are you so excited?" I ask.

Lo moves closer, placing her hand on my shoulder. "Because she listened. She heard me out. And that's got to mean something."

I passed the fountain at The Jasper again today after lunch, only this time I took a seat at one of the benches. About the time I was ready to leave, something shiny caught the corner of my eye. When I took a closer look, I spotted a quarter beneath one of the benches—the very same bench Love was standing next to the night I first met her.

Heading to my room to change out of my work clothes, I pull Love's quarter from my pocket and sit it on top of my dresser.

CHAPTER FORTY-SEVEN

LOVE

I LOCK the front door of the Agenda W building and slide my keys in my bag while Cameo orders a ride because she refuses to take the subway or walk more than a block in her pristine Louboutins.

We must have interviewed at least seven people this afternoon, one after another after another from the moment I returned from grabbing a coffee, and I never had a chance to tell her about running into Lo at Starbucks.

"Okay. Ride's going to be here in five minutes," my sister says before darkening the screen of her phone. "What'd you think of the candidates? I thought we had some good ones."

"Yeah," I say.

She studies my face, thin brows meeting as she chuckles. "Yeah? That's all you have to say?"

"I'm just tired." I amble toward a metal park bench by the curb and take a seat.

Cameo follows.

"I ran into Jude's sister earlier today," I say. "When I was getting coffee."

She rolls her eyes. "Ah. So that's why you were so out of it all afternoon. Thought maybe you were coming down with something."

"I wasn't out of it."

"Yes, Love, you were." Her voice is louder, as if that gives her opinion more weight. "You asked the same question twice in a row when we interviewed that social worker from Queens and then you called the three o'clock by the four o'clock's name."

"Oops." I glance down at my folded hands resting on my lap. I suppose I was a little off my game this afternoon. I tried to focus on the interviews, but my mind wouldn't stop replaying everything Lo said during our brief exchange at the coffee shop.

"So what'd she say?" Cameo asks, angling her body toward me as if I'm about to give her some major gossip.

Sitting up, I stare straight ahead, brows lifted. "That he's sorry. That he loves me. That he'll never forgive himself. You know, that kind of stuff."

"Do you believe her?"

I shrug my left shoulder. "I don't have a reason not to. I'm just trying to decide if how sorry he is even matters."

Cameo crosses her legs and clears her throat. "When you two were in town for the wedding, there was this night when I was sitting outside on Mom's front steps, just sort of ... reflecting, I guess you could say. Jude walked out to grab something from your car and he saw me. He could've just said hi and kept going, but he stopped and sat down and asked me if I was okay."

"He did?"

Cameo's red lips draw into a slow smile and she nods. "Yep. And Bob said when Jude went to his bachelor party, all these women were hitting on him, but he was just sitting there sipping his beer and going through his phone, looking at pictures of the two of you."

"Yeah, well it's not like he could've hooked up with anyone else ... he knows word would've traveled back to me and then his charade would be over."

Cameo rolls her eyes. "You know, one night I asked him how you two made it look like you'd been together forever and he said it was because his life didn't begin until he met you, so he feels like he's known you his whole life."

I pretend to gag myself. "He's got some great lines. I'll give him that."

"Say what you want," Cameo says, tossing her manicured hands in the air. "It was cheesy as hell, but I believed him. And there's our ride."

We leave the bench as a red Chevy Malibu with a Lyft sign on the dash pulls up to the curb, and then we climb in the backseat.

"So what are you saying?" I ask my sister. "That I should give him another chance?"

"I don't know." She glances out the window, nose wrinkling as if my question annoys her. "I can't make that decision for you."

"Would you? If you found out everything Bob ever said or did was a lie and he had the nerve to marry you anyway?"

Cameo sighs, folding her hands in her lap and staring ahead, though I think she might be checking her reflection in the driver's rearview mirror.

"Like I said, I don't know. I wish I had some better advice for you, but you know that's never been my wheelhouse," she says, all but admitting she's been a less-than-ideal big sister over the years—a first. "I just wanted to make sure you had all the facts."

Her opinions aren't "facts," but I don't tell her that. I appreciate that she's engaging in a conversation that doesn't revolve around her. This is a rare and special moment between us, and Dad would be proud.

"Aren't there literally millions of men out here? Surely you can find someone else," she muses. "Either stop dwelling on him and move on or find someone new."

She makes it sound like handbag shopping, like a replacement is one taxi cab ride and a credit card swipe away.

"Hunter made him sign an NDA, I guess," I say as we cross the Brooklyn Bridge. "He's legally not allowed to tell me anything or talk about the terms of the agreement to anyone."

Turning toward me, she says, "You know, Bob's brother is a family law attorney. Let me text him."

Cameo digs her phone out from the bottom of her Dior bag and fires off a text. A minute later, her phone dings.

"A-ha." She brings the phone closer, smiling like a high school mean girl who just stumbled upon some damning intel. "He says, *'This could fall under spousal support fraud, which usually pertains to people lying about their income or job status to reduce their financial obligations, but it can be a gray area and it's definitely worth looking into. If she needs any recommendations, I know some good family law attorneys in New York.'*"

"Knowing Hunter, he probably had the NDA drafted carefully and strategically so he's fully protected. He's slimy like that." And undeniably savvy, which is how he got to where he is today.

"Maybe ... Give me two seconds." She fires off another text, her nails clicking against the screen. And a moment later, he responds. "Yes!"

"What?"

"*Under certain circumstances, if the NDA pertains to illegal activity, it becomes null and void and cannot be enforced,*" she says, reading his message. "*If your sister's ex-husband's arrangement falls under spousal support fraud, the NDA cannot be enforced and the signee of the NDA is free to report and/or testify.*"

"Yeah, but you'd think Hunter would know that," I say, face tightening into an incredulous glare. "It doesn't make sense. He's smart. He wouldn't put himself at risk like that."

"I've never known anything to stop Hunter from getting what he wants. Have you?" she asks. "Maybe the reward outweighed the risk?"

Sighing, I say, "Yeah. I could see that."

I could also see him thinking his wealth made him immune to the law.

"So this is good, right? If the NDA doesn't hold, that means you can talk to Jude about *everything*," she says.

"It doesn't change anything though. It doesn't justify what he did. I think ... I think I just need to let this go," I say the words I've been telling myself every single day for weeks now. They've yet to sink in.

"Do you miss him?"

The car pulls up outside The Jasper and Cameo pays the tab on her phone before we climb out and stand beneath the black awning outside the entrance.

I try to answer her, only I can't.

"You hesitated," she says, pointing at me. "That's a yes."

"Look. We had fun together. And I miss the fun we had when I thought it was real and that he liked me, but—"

"—Love, it *was* real," she cuts me off, eyes rolling yet again. "The pretenses might have been false, but he liked you. It was written all over his face the week of the wedding. I saw it every time he looked at you, every time he put his hand on the small of your back or brushed your hair out of your eyes or kissed you on your forehead for no reason."

I squint, trying to wrap my head around the fact that my sister was able to see any of that when she was stuck inside her Bridezilla bubble.

Maybe I don't give her enough credit sometimes ...

"And all those embarrassing stories I shared? I was testing him. And Love ... he passed." She chuckles, like she's so proud of her prowess. "Bet you thought I was just being a brat."

"Amongst other things."

Cameo nudges me with a lanky elbow. "I know we haven't always had a perfect relationship and we couldn't be more different, but you're my little sister and you've always been there for me, and believe it or not, I care about you."

Our matching eyes hold, and I can't decide if I'm touched or weirded out by this Hallmark moment.

"This feels ... unnatural," I say.

Cameo's serious expression fades and she bursts into laughter. "Extremely. Anyway, I'm going to head to my hotel because I'm exhausted, but call me if you need anything."

"Thanks, Cam." I give her a wave because I think we're both still too weirded out to hug right now, and I watch as her heels clip up the sidewalk, making the short walk to The Peninsula Hotel.

Heading inside, I stop first and take a detour toward the other side of the building, stopping at the fountain in the courtyard for no reason other than I'm not quite in the mood to hole up for the night yet.

Taking a seat on an empty bench, I listen to the trickle of the water, wishing my dad were here so I could ask him what he thinks. He was always so good with relationships, his advice always heartfelt yet practical and always perfect.

Pulling my bag over my head, I place it beside me and cross my legs. I don't know how long I plan to stay here, but I've got nowhere else to be so it doesn't matter anyway. A few moment later, I realize I'm sitting on the very bench I lost my quarter under the night I met Jude, but I don't search for it.

It's got to be long gone.

Just like everything else.

Drawing in a balmy, summer's breath, I think back to our last full day together before I was smacked upside the head with the truth. We were flying back from West Virginia and our flight was delayed six hours due to mechanical problems. Under any other circumstances, it would've put a damper in my day, but I didn't think twice about it because I just remember thinking I could be anywhere with Jude and still find a way to enjoy it.

We spent those listless hours playing Mad Libs, eating Starbursts, and reading magazines. In the middle of the afternoon, he bought a Cinnabon and let me have the middle. When we finally loaded onto our plane a lifetime later, I realized I'd lost my earbuds. He gave me one of his over the course of our flight, introduced me to some of the most incredible bands I never knew existed.

Every time I looked at him that day, I just remember thinking, "How did I get so lucky?"

The shuffle of footsteps heading toward the courtyard places me back here, firmly planted in a reality where those moments are no longer relevant.

A young couple saunter up to the fountain, and the man digs into his pocket for some change.

"What are you going to wish for?" he asks, placing a shiny quarter in her hand.

I leave.

CHAPTER FORTY-EIGHT

JUDE

IT'S our last day on site at Lenox Hill. Next assignment will be some apartment building being renovated in the Meat Packing District, so I won't be in Love's neighborhood after today.

For the past couple of weeks, I kept hoping I'd run into her one more time, but our paths never crossed—just like they were probably never meant to cross in the first place.

Heading back from the deli on my lunch break, I stop at the fountain by The Jasper one last time. This morning when I was getting ready for work and realizing it was going to be my last day on this job, I grabbed Love's quarter off my dresser and dropped it in my pocket.

I've never been a nostalgic person. I've never been one to hold onto material things and give them some kind of value based on whether or not they once belonged to someone ... but this quarter is different. It represents mistakes. Heartbreak and fear, joy and loss, hope. But mostly it represents Love, and I need to let it go.

Approaching the west side of the fountain, I spot a small plaque on the side that I never noticed before. The inscription reads, *"A man, when he wishes, is the master of his fate."*

I don't know about that, but at this point, I have nothing to lose. Sliding the quarter from my pocket, I twist the coin between the pads of my fingers, trying to convince myself to toss it in and watch it sink to the bottom.

But I can't.

———

THE APARTMENT IS UNUSUALLY quiet for a Friday night, and I find a note on the kitchen table from Lo, letting me know she took the girls to the park. She's got every other weekend off, so I don't have to babysit the girls tonight.

A bunch of guys from work invited me out tonight for beer and the sports bar down the street is playing the Mets game, so I might stop there on the way.

I make my way to my room and strip out of my work clothes, tossing them into a plastic hamper in the corner next to my guitars—the ones I haven't touched in weeks. I haven't had the urge to play since I left The Jasper, and sometimes I worry if it'll ever come back.

I've thought about writing a million songs about Love, but it wouldn't feel right exploiting her all over again, and for what? So every record company in New York can slam their doors in my face the second they realize who I am?

Changing into a pair of clean jeans from a laundry basket on my bed, I locate an old Cure t-shirt and tug it over my head. I stop at the kitchen next, grabbing an Old Milwaukee from the fridge before settling into an armchair in the living room and flicking the TV on for the sake of not being alone with my thoughts.

Three knocks at the door twenty minutes later nearly cause me to spit my beer out.

Fucking solicitors.

People are always coming through here, sliding their takeout menus under our doors or trying to sell candy bars for their shady fundraisers.

I turn up the volume on the TV and wait for them to leave.

Only they knock again.

And again.

"Not home!" I yell, shaking my head and taking another swig.

The asshole on the other side of the door chooses to ignore me, knocking again, only harder this time. Muting the TV, I slam the remote down, sit my beer on the coffee table, and get up from the chair, fully prepared to give this menu-slinging neckbeard a piece of my mind, only when I jerk the door open, I'm met with a familiar honey gaze.

"Love ..." My hand lifts to my messy hair, and I remember that I look like shit.

"Mind if I come in?" she asks. She isn't smiling and her tone is flat. A pencil skirt and short-sleeved blouse cover her body, and loose blonde curls frame her face. The smallest part of me hopes to God she just left work and she's not on her way to some date.

"What is this? Why are you here?"

"Can I come in?" Love asks again, glancing past my shoulder then back to me.

"Yeah, yeah." I step aside and let her in, hoping to God

no one saw her come here. "You, uh, want something to drink?"

Her lips form a straight line and she exhales through her nose. "No thank you. I won't be staying long."

Hooking my hands on my hips, I give her my full attention.

"I just came here to ask you one question," she says, clearing her throat. Her eyes shift from mine to the floor and back, and she keeps her left hand clutched tight around the strap of her black purse.

"Anything," I say.

"Why?" she asks. "Why did you do it? And why didn't you stop when it got real?"

"I want to tell you that, Love. I really do. I'd give anything to be able to answer those for you, but I—"

"I know about the NDA," she says. "And I've consulted with an attorney who assured me any contract related to illegal activities is unenforceable."

"The contract wasn't related to the agreement—it was just a general NDA that prevents me from talking to anyone about anything Hunter and I have spoken about." I lifting my hand to the scorching skin on my neck for a second. "He made sure nothing else was put into writing. I don't even think there would be a way to prove any of—"

"Marissa," she says. "His assistant. She overheard everything you two discussed the first time you met."

My brows meet, and I think back to that day, when we were alone in the office. "How?"

"He accidentally dialed her," she says. "Anyway, she heard it all. And she's the one who told me everything last month, the day after we got back from Cameo's wedding."

I search her eyes for a moment. "So that day, when you disappeared and you said you had the migraine ..."

"I was avoiding you, yes."

I don't blame her, nor do I hold it against her.

"I was going to tell you that day." My throat constricts. "We'd spent that week together and it was honestly, Love, one of the better weeks of my life. And I realized as soon as we got back, that this was becoming real, and I realized I couldn't hurt you. Not the way I was supposed to. So I was going to tell you the next day ... but you were unreachable. And the next day you showed up with a smile on your face, saying you wanted to spend the day together and that you missed me, and I selfishly gave myself one more day with you." I exhale, shaking my head. "And then the thing with Piper happened. And you left for The Hamptons the next day." Massaging the back of my neck, I continue, "I went to Hunter when you were gone. I told him I couldn't do this anymore. He told me I had a week to leave the apartment, so I was going to tell you as soon as you got back, but the day before that, I came back from a run and he was there, waiting for me. He doubled his offer. And then he more than doubled *that* offer. When I still wouldn't budge, he demanded my key and my phone and had me blacklisted from the building."

The storm in Love's honey eyes allays, but only slightly.

"I was going to tell you," I say. "I wanted to be the one. And it killed me that you thought I went radio silent on you, that you thought I abandoned you like a fucking coward."

Her eyes snap to the floor and her shoulders shake as she inhales. What I wouldn't give to take her in my arms ...

"Everything blew up in my face." I slide my hands into the front pockets of my jeans. All they want to do is touch her, her hair, her skin, her lips—and I don't trust myself. "I think about you every day, Love." My whisper breaks. "I miss you all the time."

I miss her greedy hands grabbing on me when I'm trying to brush my teeth in the morning.

I miss the warmth of her body formed against mine under the icy cool sheets of my bed.

I miss her infectious laugh. The dimples above her perfect, peach-shaped ass. I miss the half-moon shaped spray of freckles on her left arm.

Love's silence is concerning, her icy demeanor evident in the space she maintains between us and her refusal to offer a semblance of sentence, but I can't be upset with her.

I have no right.

"You still haven't told me why." Her eyes search mine as she clears her throat, and her hands are clasped in front of her, knuckles white.

"Because I'm a piece of shit loser." I half chuckle. She doesn't. "Listen, Love. I didn't have some idyllic childhood in some cutesy little town. I didn't have a mom and dad who gave two shits about me. All I had was my kid sister and whatever relative-of-the-month wanted to take us in."

She begins to say something, but I stop her.

"I'm not asking for your sympathy," I continue. "I'm just answering your question. My entire life, I've been in survival mode. I've always done what I needed to do. And in this case, I needed to take care of my sister and my nieces. Piper was sick. I'd just lost my job. We were all on the verge of being fucking homeless and then I had this rich asshole promising me to answer every prayer I'd ever made if I did him this one little favor ..."

Love's stare moves to her feet.

I wish she'd give me a sign. I wish she'd say something instead of letting me babble on like the pathetic, desperate-to-win-her-back idiot that I am.

"I was in the army," I say. I don't know why I feel the

need to tell her this. Maybe it's because it's a piece of who I am and all I've done is give her pieces of who I thought she wanted me to be. "Enlisted after high school graduation. Was a mechanic, but the military life wasn't for me. After that I taught myself guitar, wrote a few songs, played in bars whenever I could, and I worked a shit ton of dead end jobs until someone lined me up with a plumbing apprenticeship. That's what I was doing until ... recently."

She doesn't blink, doesn't shift her posture. I couldn't read her if I tried.

"Look, I'll stop rambling. And I know my word is shit," I say. "I know you have no reason to believe a single thing I say. But I just want you to know—"

"I have to go," she says, pushing past me and marching toward the door. Her eyes are glassy, but her expression is cold.

"Wait," I say as she grabs the door knob.

Love doesn't wait, and I follow her into the hall where the air is hot and stale and scented like oregano. Nothing about this moment is romantic. It's not a scene from a movie. It's real life, and real life can be ugly and suffocating and uncomfortable sometimes.

"Can I ask you one question?" I keep back a few feet, giving her space and trying to respect that she doesn't want to be here anymore.

Love stops, turning to glance back at me, her eyes examining mine. I wait for her to speak, to say anything at all, but all I hear is a screaming baby from the apartment next door and a man yelling at his wife to "Shut that kid up or I will!"

"I have to go," she finally says.

And I let her go. With burning eyes and a cannon-sized hole in my chest, I watch her walk away from me.

I don't chase her or cause a scene, because she means too much to me and I've already done enough.

And besides, she deserves better.

CHAPTER FORTY-NINE

LOVE

I'VE ALWAYS LOVED the way the city empties out on Saturdays. Things are a little less crowded and chaotic and a little more peaceful. There's more room to breathe, the locals a little less agitated.

Stopping by a flower cart on my way back from grabbing coffee, I pick a bouquet of dark pink peonies—some of the last of the season since fall's not too far off. Peonies are the kind of flowers you have to enjoy while you can because they don't bloom all year and they never last very long once they've been cut from their vine, but my God, are they a fragrant thing of beauty in their prime.

"Thank you." I hand the man behind the cart a twenty and he hands me my flowers wrapped in brown paper.

Balancing the flowers under one arm, my bag over my shoulder, and my coffee in my free hand, I feel my phone vibrating in my pocket and somehow manage to grab it.

The number across the screen is unfamiliar, though I recognize the New York area code. For a moment, the most miniscule part of me wonders if it's Jude, though after the way I stormed out of his apartment and ignored his request to ask me a question last night, I can't imagine he'd turn around and call me up the very next morning.

Sliding my thumb across the bottom of the screen, I clear my throat and answer.

"Hello?"

"Love?" the man's voice says on the other end. I don't know who this is, but it only takes an instant for me to know who it isn't.

"This is she." I tuck my flowers tight beneath my arm and trek home.

"It's Sascha," he says, his accent more apparent. "From The Hamptons."

"Yes, I remember. How are you?" My tone is more cordial and formal than it should be. But I never expected him to actually call and truth be told, I was perfectly fine with that.

Sascha, in all his exotic beauty and unabashed interest, doesn't do it for me.

"I'm very well," he says. "Yourself?"

I stifle a yawn. "Doing well."

"I'm coming back to the city this week. Wanted to see if you had any plans for Friday night?"

"Oh. Um." I struggle to find the best way to turn him down. The mere thought of going on a date with him already feels like an obligation, and I haven't even said yes.

"I thought maybe I'd cook us dinner at my place," he says. "Then we could go out on the roof, watch the stars."

He's trying too hard, which is a shame because he doesn't need to. By all accounts, Sascha is a catch. But I can't help but feel that much more turned off. It doesn't matter anyway. There's nothing he could or couldn't do to change the truth I'm too terrified to admit out loud: he's not the one that I want.

"Can I let you know tomorrow?" I ask, praying I can buy some time to come up with a way to let him down gently. Or who knows ... maybe I'll get a wild hair and change my mind between now and then?

"Yeah. Sure. Tomorrow would be fine," he says, his disappointment evident in the way he pauses between words.

"Perfect. I'll call you then."

By the time I get back to my apartment, I trim the stems of my peonies and place them in a vase of water on my kitchen island. The dark pink stands out against all the silver and white, bringing its unapologetic vivacity into a space that was formerly lifeless.

When I'm finished, I grab my phone to text Tierney because I promised her I'd stop by today to see the baby. But before I have a chance to compose a message, there's a knock at my door.

Freezing in place, I listen again, wondering if maybe it was the door across the hall—Jude's old place. I saw that a young couple moved in last weekend. They might have visitors?

Returning my attention to my phone, I begin to tap out a text, only the knocks return—louder now and unmistakably coming from my door. Placing my phone on the counter, I shuffle to the door, palms hot and splayed on the door as I rise on my toes to peer through the peephole.

It only takes a second for me to realize exactly who's standing on the other side of my door. A warmth blooms in my cheeks and my heart flutters. I try to tell my body to calm down, but it won't listen.

Pulling the door open a second later, I wipe all signs of emotion from my expression and lock eyes on his.

"Yes?" I ask.

"You came to my door yesterday, demanding an answer to the one question that'd been eating you up inside," he says, "and now it's my turn."

Last night when I was trying to leave, when I felt a wave of tears beginning to crest and threaten to crash over me, I bolted out of there. I'd yet to cry over him and I refused to let the first time be right there, standing in his living room after I'd managed to keep a brave front until then.

Pulling in a sharp breath, I explore his dusty green irises, feeling the swell in my chest and the twist in my stomach all at once.

"Fine," I say. I don't invite him in.

Jude licks his full lips, his eyes capturing mine. "When you told me you loved me that day ... did you mean it?"

I hesitate, and when I try to answer, the right words escape me.

"Did you mean it, Love?" he asks again, chin slightly tucked and words spoken quickly, as if to lend a sense of urgency to his question.

I didn't mean it at the time.

But after some time had passed, after my heart had been tugged in every which direction, I realized there was a part of me that was beginning to fall in love with him before it all fell apart.

My chest rises and falls, and I swallow the lump in my throat before answering him.

"No," I say.

Jude exhales, his shoulders straightening and the

space above his jaw flexing. He studies me a moment longer, his stare intense, like this is the last time he's ever going to see me and he wants to ingrain this into his memory.

"That's all I needed to know," he says a few seconds later. "Goodbye, Love."

Before I have a chance to say anything, he's already halfway down the hall. I don't stick around to watch him step into the elevator. Instead, I return inside and lock the door, resting my back against it when I realize my chest is so tight it hurts to breathe.

It's over now, this time for good, but I thought it would feel different. I thought I'd feel lighter. Instead, there's this gnawing emptiness, like a vacant cavity where my heart should be. All that hurt and animosity has taken a back burner.

Rushing to the living room window, I press my fingers on the glass and watch for him to come out from beneath the awning.

A minute passes, then another, and eventually five.

He should've left the building by now.

I'm not sure how he got in here in the first place, given the fact that he claimed to be blacklisted, but maybe someone noticed him? Or maybe he had to sneak out through the courtyard exit?

Either way, he's gone, and still, I can't bring myself to step away from the window on the off chance I might see him one *more* last time.

My hands tremble and my mind grows loud, recalling all the things Lo said, the things Cameo shared with me, the forlorn look in Jude's eyes every time he's apologized to me. When he told me last night that he misses me every day, that he thinks about me all the time, I didn't let those works soak in then, but I close my eyes and hear them all over again.

And when I finally accept that I feel the same way, I find the answer I've been searching for this entire time: I can hate what he did, but I don't have to hate him.

I know, now, what I need to do.

CHAPTER FIFTY

JUDE

LOVE'S QUARTER is sandwiched between my thumb and forefinger, the metal still warm from my pocket. Sitting at a park bench by the fountain, I watch the water spill over the top of the marble umbrella, and I take in the view of the smiling, rain-drenched couple one last time.

I came here for an answer, and that's exactly what she gave me.

It's time to let her go. And honestly? She was never mine to have in the first place.

Rising, I make my way to closer to the rippling waters and lift my hand. With a quick snap of a wrist, I let it go, watching as it lands with a gentle plunk before sinking to the bottom with all the others.

"What'd you wish for?" A woman's voice asks from behind.

Turning, I find Love standing next to the bench where I first found her.

"Nothing," I say.

Tucking a strand of yellow hair behind her ear, she takes a step closer. "So you were just ... throwing money into a fountain ... for no reason?"

I can't take my eyes off her, glued to her every move, every twitch of her lips and every flick of her hazel eyes.

"Basically," I say, my gaze dropping to her right hand, where I realize she's worrying her thumb against something small and shiny. "What is this? What are we doing?"

She closes the space between us, her sweet perfume trailing into my lungs. I let it linger as I resist the urge to cup her fair cheek in my hand and have my way with her pillowed lips all over again.

"When I was with you," she says, "I felt like I could finally be myself for the first time in my life. And it was liberating. Freedom like I'd never known. And on top of that? You made me feel smart and sexy and pretty and funny and all the things I've always wanted to feel. Every day with you was better than the one before. So easy. So natural. I'd fall asleep with butterflies in my stomach and wake up with a smile on my face. But the you hurt me." Her gaze falls to the coin in her hands. "More than anyone has *ever* hurt me." Drawing in a hard breath, her golden stare snaps onto mine. "But I didn't come down here to lecture you."

"Then why'd you come?"

Love flattens her palm, lifting it higher to show me the quarter. "I came down here to make a wish."

"Says the girl who doesn't believe in wishes."

She rolls her eyes, biting back a smirk. "I know."

"Don't let me stop you." I move out of the way, ensuring her path to the fountain is unobstructed.

Love readies her toss, focused ahead, but she stops, turning back to me. "Before I do this, I just wanted to tell you ... when I said I loved you, I didn't mean it ... then. But before that? Before everything came crashing down? I knew it was coming. I was standing on that ledge, a single push away from falling."

Her eyes close, wincing for a moment.

"I wish I could hate you, Jude," she says. "I wish I could tell myself that I never want to see you again and actually believe it. But the truth is, I think about you every day. And maybe I shouldn't, but I do, and I think about what you said, what your sister said, what my sister said ... and that's why I feel like ... maybe ... maybe we could try this again?"

Her words, as unexpected as they are, bring an instant fullness where the void in my chest used to be.

Moving closer, I cup her cheek, the way I've been dying to do every time I've seen her, but the second I remember the NDA, celebrating feels premature.

"You know if Hunter sees us together ..." I say, not wanting to finish my thought.

"I can call my lawyer first thing Monday so we can work on filing charges and voiding your contract." Love bites her lip for a moment, and I wonder if she feels the charge between us the same way I do. "If you want to fight this, that is ..."

Fighting this is the only way we can be together without the past lingering over us like a dark cloud, without the threat of Hunter lurking around the corner waiting to make a mess of the shattered remnants before we have a chance to glue all the pieces back together.

Sliding my palm along her jaw, until my fingers are

buried in her hair, I lower my mouth to hers.

"Like hell," I say. "We'll fight like hell."

Grazing my lips against hers, I taste her mouth, slow and lingering, before stealing a kiss. A moment later, I slide my hands to her waist, hooking around the small of her back and pressing her against me. Love sighs before she melts in my arms, and our tongues dance to the sound of the trickling fountain that started it all.

"You have no idea how happy you've made me," I whisper into her ear before pressing kisses down the side of her neck.

There are a hundred other ways I want to show her my appreciation, but none of them are exactly courtyard appropriate.

As if she's reading my mind, Love slips away, tucking her hand into mine, and leading me back inside The Jasper. A woman with a small dog in a designer bag waits by the elevator, sunglasses covering her eyes and her nose lifted in the air. It takes all the strength I have to restrain myself, but somehow, I manage. When the lady climbs out on the fourth floor, Love and I find ourselves alone, and the moment the elevator doors close, she's all mine again.

Pulling her close, I slide my hands down her thighs and lift her into my arms. Her legs wrap around my hips as she cups my face, her mouth twisted at the sides and red from my kiss. Within seconds, we arrive on her floor, but I don't let her go.

Carrying her down the hall, I press her back against her door once we arrive and taste the soft flesh of her neck.

"Keys, Love," I whisper, my lips pressed against her skin.

"What?"

"Your keys," I say, my voice low. "I can't wait another

minute. I have to have you right fucking now."

She slides down my body, her back still pressed against the door, and when her feet reach the ground, she digs into her pocket and retrieves her key. While she works the lock, I wrap my hands around her waist, fingers teasing at the waistband of her jeans as she squirms against me.

A decade later, we're finally inside and all bets are off.

Slamming the door behind me, I follow Love as she walks backward toward her room, peeling her shirt over her head and tossing it aside, followed by her black lace bra. By the time she works the button of her jeans, we've reached the doorway.

By the time she backs into the bed, she's completely naked, her body on full display like the work of fucking art that it is.

Love slides onto the center of the bed, lying on her back, and I unfasten my jeans and slide them down before climbing over her and spreading her thighs. Running my fingertips along her delicate seam, I tease and circle before lowering myself to get a taste.

She's sweet and soft, wet for me, and hot to the touch, and my God, she's all mine.

When I've had my fill and she's breathless and staggering on the edge of a long overdue climax, I grab a rubber from her nightstand where we used to keep them and climb over her again, running my palm along her outer thigh.

Love reaches for me, tracing the peaks and valleys along my abs before digging her nails into the flesh on my hips and pushing me against her.

She grinds against me like the tease she loves to be, and my cock throbs. Slicked in her arousal, I reach down, gripping my aching cock and teasing her clit until she squirms beneath me and begs for the real thing.

Grabbing the rubber beside us, I rip the packet between my teeth and slide it down before lifting her legs over my shoulders. Love's breathless sighs turn into moans the second I enter her, filling her to the hilt with every inch of me.

I'm not used to being so animalistic with her, but that wild look in her golden gaze tells me she doesn't mind a bit. I think we both needed to get this out of our system ... we need one night of hair-pulling, clothes-ripping, lip-biting sex.

Plunging my length into her again and again, faster and harder, I hold her thighs and drive myself deeper, steadying my rhythm as I watch for the rake of her teeth against her lips—her tell. A moment later, Love's hips buck against my thrusts as she comes, and I lose myself in my own release.

Collapsing beside her, our bodies hot and sticky, I brush the hair from her eyes before tracing her swollen mouth with my thumb.

"I missed that so much," she said, exhaling as if it was some secret she'd been harboring.

"You have no idea," I say, leaning in to steal a kiss.

"But," she says, pulling away. Her hair spills down her shoulder. "I have one request."

"Anything."

"After tonight ... after we do what we're going to do ... can we take things slow?" she asks, one brow higher than the other. "I want to go slow. I want to enjoy this."

My mouth lifts in one corner as I drink in her beautiful glow in the warm daylight that filters through her window.

"We'll go as slow as you want. I've got all the time in the world." Whatever it takes, whatever I have to do ... I'll do it.

Love slides closer, cozying beneath my arm and pressing her cheek against my racing heart.

"Jude?"

"Yeah?"

"How'd you get in the building earlier ... I thought you were blacklisted?" she asks.

Staring at the ceiling, I run my fingers through her hair and smirk. "I did some work for Raymond last month. Installed new faucets in his bathroom and kitchen and replaced a p-trap. He owed me a favor. I called it in."

"Wow." She laughs through her nose, tracing her nails down the center of my chest. "Wait ... so are you a plumber?"

"I am."

Love sits up on her elbow studying me.

"Is ... that a problem?" I ask.

Her brows knit, and I can't tell if she's thinking or if she's angry.

"No," she says a moment later, biting her lip until it grows pinker. "I think it's really freaking sexy that you can fix things around the house."

"You do?"

Love nods.

"Did I tell you I was a mechanic in the Army back in the day?" I add.

"Staaahp!" Her eyes roll to the back of her head. "That's so damn hot."

I start to tell her about all the other things I can fix ... radios, guitars, small kitchen appliances ... but she shuts me up with a kiss, her lips hot like fire against mine.

A second later, she's climbing over me, straddling my hips, her wetness teasing my growing hardness with a slow grind. "Think I'm ready for an encore, Jude Warner."

"Anything you want."

I'd give this girl the world if she asked.

EPILOGUE

JUDE

ONE YEAR LATER

I THOUGHT a trip home would be a nice distraction for her, so I booked our flights and surprised her on a random Wednesday. Just so happened to be her mom's birthday and Cameo's baby shower, so it all worked out.

Love's phone has been blowing up the past few weeks as Hunter awaits arraignment for his spousal support fraud charges. The media is dying to hear what she has to say, but she won't give them a single soundbite, always opting with a tried-and-true, "No comment."

The papers have been blasting him, painting him in a horrible light with a side of the most unflattering pictures they can dig up on the bastard. He looks like a deer in headlights in every one of them, always putting his hands out as he makes his way to his limousine from whatever *chi chi* eatery he still frequents.

The board at Blue Stream Records wasted no time voting him out. That kind of publicity could bankrupt them, because all their musical acts would utilize the clause in their contracts specifically linked to bad behavior on either side.

Personally, I think it's fucking hilarious.

And all of this because he couldn't bear to part with a small fraction of his riches. I don't even want to guess what he's spending on legal fees right now.

Some news outlets are speculating that his net worth is plummeting by the second, though I'm not sure where they're getting that information. And Love isn't the slightest bit worried. She has more than enough set aside and more than enough left over from the past year to keep Agenda W flourishing.

Thank God no one's come looking for me yet. Love's attorney managed to negotiate to get me immunity for testifying against him. So far, my name hasn't come up yet, but if this goes to trial, there's a chance it could.

Love assures me it's a non-issue for her.

Three nights ago, we arrived in Sweet Water. Yesterday was cake and ice cream. The day before that was Cameo's baby shower since she and Bob are expecting a little girl any day now. Today we've spent the morning ambling around town, stopping into quaint shops and little cafes where everyone seems to know exactly who Love is. Their faces light the second they see her come in, and they all try to talk her ear off.

Just an hour ago, we stepped into a little antique shop on Walnut Road. The owner kept leading us toward the jewelry case, and Love didn't say much, but I saw her gaze wander toward a silver ring with a milky pearl stone in the middle and a halo of diamonds around it.

The owner told us it once belonged to the wife of the town's founder, who managed to keep it in the family for a couple of generations until the Great Depression hit. After that, the ring bounced from local family to local family, but it always seemed to come back.

"That's too bad," Love said. "It's so pretty. It deserves a good home."

"That it does," the owner said to her as he winked at me.

I waited until she sauntered off to some corner of the shop filled with vintage china sets before slipping the guy some cash. He counted it out, nodded, and then quietly took the ring out from its case and polished it with a dry cloth. A moment later, he slipped it into a small wooden box with navy blue velvet inside. When we were both sure she wasn't looking, he slid it across the glass counter, and I shoved it in my pocket.

We've only been together (officially) a year, but already I know I want to spend the rest of my life with this woman. But if I married her, she'd lose her alimony—assuming there's much of anything left after his trial and all the negative publicity, and I wouldn't do that to her or to her business. Things have been going exceedingly well for Agenda W this past year. So well, in fact, that she plans to open sister locations in each of the boroughs over the next five years.

"Oh! There's the fountain I wanted to show you," Love pulls me across a blacktop street toward a sculpture of what appears to be a bronze mermaid. "It wasn't here last time. I guess they share it with some town in Denmark? Anyway, this is based on Hans Christian Andersen's Little Mermaid.

My dad used to take me here all the time for coin tossing contests when I was a kid."

Love's radiant eyes match the wide beam claiming her face.

"Ten points for hitting her tail. Twenty for the seashell necklace," she says, moving closer to the fountain. Stooping low, she scoops her hand across the top of the water, like she couldn't resist. A moment later, she turns back toward me. "Hey, do you have any—" Love's hands cup her gaping mouth. "What is ... what is this? What are you doing?"

Her gaze turns glassy as she takes two steps toward me, then another, and another.

"This isn't a marriage proposal," I say, despite the fact that I'm down on one knee with a ring box propped in my hand.

"Okay?" She's laughing and crying, her hands flitting around her face. "What are you doing?"

"I'm not asking you to marry me, Love. I'm asking you to spend the rest of your life with me." My chest swells and my throat is tight, but I carry on. "I don't care about labels and papers. I don't care about making it legal or official. All I care about is you. Nothing more. Nothing less. So will you spend the rest of your life with me?"

Her tear-brimmed eyes move toward the pearl ring resting in the wooden case in my hand, and she takes it from me.

"When did you ... how did you?"

"I never knew how adorable you are when you get flustered." I wink. "So what do you say?"

She slips the vintage jewel over her left ring finger with ease, and I rise, towering over her and pulling her into my arms.

"So is that a yes?" I ask.

Rising on her toes, she cups my face in her sweet hands and kisses me soft and slow, like she never wants this moment to end.

"That's a yes."

THE END

DREAM CAST

Love Aldridge – Michelle Williams
Jude Warner – Justin Hartley
Tierney Castle – JoAnna Garcia
Lo Warner – Emma Stone
Hunter LeGrand – Josh Henderson
Cameo Aldridge – Beth Behrs

SNEAK PEEK OF P.S. I MISS YOU

*Unedited and subject to change

Chapter One

Melrose

I've been a dog-walker on an episode of Will & Grace.

A bakery shop owner in a Lifetime movie.

Ryan Gosling's kid sister in an indie flick that never saw the light of day.

Victim #2 in a season eighteen episode of Law & Order: SVU.

But today I'm faced with my most challenging role yet; a camera-less reality show called *Girl with Lifelong Crush on Best Guy Friend* starring Melrose Claiborne as ... Melrose Claiborne.

Standing outside Nick Camden's Studio City bungalow, I straighten my shoulders, smooth my blonde waves into place, and reach for the doorbell. The heavy thump of my heart suggests it's going to fall to the floor the second he opens the door—but I'm hopeful the butterflies in my stomach will catch it first.

He has this effect on me.

Every. Single. Time.

And that's saying something because it takes a lot to make me nervous, to throw me off my game. But my crush on him has only intensified over the years, growing stronger with each unrequited year that passes.

But last night, out of nowhere, Nick called me—which was strange because Nick never calls. He only ever texts. He's so against calling, in fact, that he has his ringer permanently set to "off" and his voicemail box has been full for the last six and a half years.

"Mel, I need to talk to you tomorrow," he'd said, breathless almost. There was a hint of a smile in his tone, giddiness. "It's *really* important."

"Nick, you're scaring me," I told him, half wondering if someone slipped something into his drink and he was drugged out of his mind. "What's this about?"

"I have to tell you in person. And I have something to ask you, something crazy important," he said. "Oh, my god. This is insane. I'm so fucking nervous, Mel. But as soon as you get here tomorrow, I'll tell you. I've been wanting to tell you about this for a long time, but I couldn't. I couldn't until now. But now I can. And I can't fucking wait. This is huge, Mel. This is ... oh, God."

"Nick ..." I paced my bedroom floor, my left palm

clasped across my forehead. In nearly two decades of friendship, I'd never heard Nick so worked up before. "Can't you just tell me now?"

"Come over tomorrow. Around three," he'd said. "This is something that needs to be done in person."

I ring his doorbell again before checking the time on my phone. Stifling a yawn, I rise on my toes and try to peek inside the glass sidelights of his front door. Knowing Nick, he probably got side-tracked or ran out for burritos and got caught up in conversation with someone he knows.

Then again ... he was pretty insistent about talking to me in person at three o'clock about this "major" thing. I can't imagine he'd space this off.

All night, I tossed and turned, trying to wrap my head around what this could possibly be, how I could know someone for so long and fail miserably trying to get a read on them.

Growing up Nick lived next door and the two of us were inseparable from the day he first moved into the neighborhood and I found him by the creek trying to catch bullfrogs—which I promptly forced him to set free. By the end of the day, we both realized our bedroom windows aligned perfectly on the second floors of our houses, and by the end of the week, he gave me a walkie-talkie and told me I was his best friend.

When we were ten, he gave me a friendship necklace—like the kind girls usually give to other girls. He gave me the half that said "best" and wore the "friend" half but always tucked under his shirt so no one would give him any shit—not that anyone would.

Everyone loved Nick.

It wasn't until the summer after seventh grade that Nick hit a growth spurt and everything changed. His voice got deeper. His legs got longer. Even his features became more chiseled and defined. It was like he aged several years over the course of a couple of months, and I found myself looking at him in ways I never had before. And when I closed my eyes at night, I found myself thinking about what it'd be like if he kissed me.

Almost overnight, I'd gone from running next door with a messy pony tail to see if he wanted to ride bikes … to slicking on an extra coat of Dr. Pepper Lip Smackers and running a brush through my hair any time I knew I was going to see him.

Suddenly I couldn't look at him without blushing.

Unfortunately, I wasn't the only one who noticed Nick's head-turning transformation.

Nick's door swings open with a quick creak and I don't have time to realize what's happening before he sweeps me into his arms and swings me around the front porch of his rented bungalow.

"Melly!" He buries his face into my shoulder, squeezing me so hard I can't breathe, nearly suffocating the swarm of butterflies in my middle.

I breathe in that perpetual Nick scent, the one that always feels like home. Like the faintest hint of bar smoke and cheap fabric softener and Irish Spring soap. Growing up in Brentwood, the son of a successful screenwriter and composer, Nick could've had it all—materially and professionally. His parents had connections up the wazoo.

But all he ever wanted was to be a regular guy who got by on merit and I *adored* that about him.

"Look at you," he says when he puts me down. His hands are threaded in mine as his deep blue gaze scan me from head to toe. "I haven't seen you in months."

Three months, two weeks, and five days—but who's counting?

The last time we hung out was on my birthday, and there were so many people at the bar, I barely had a chance to say more than two sentences to him all night. We'd made plans to get together the following weekend, but his band booked a gig in Vegas and I was leaving to film a Lifetime movie in Vancouver the day before he was coming back.

Life's been consistent that way, always pulling us in separate directions at the most inconvenient of times.

"You find the place all right?" he asks as he leads me inside. The scent of Windex and clean laundry fills my lungs and a folded blanket rests over the back of a leather chair in the living room.

I chuckle at the thought of Nick tidying up before I got here. He was always a slob growing up. Case in point? One year I tripped over a pair of his Chucks as I entered his bedroom and almost knocked my front teeth out on a messy stack of vinyl records. His empty guitar case caught my fall, but the next day he bought a shoe organizer.

"I did," I say, glancing around his new digs. Last time I saw him, he was living in some apartment with four roommates in Toluca Lake. The time before that he was shacking up with a fuck buddy-slash-Instagram model named Kadence St. Kilda, but that was short lived because the girl ultimately wanted exclusivity and that's something Nick's never been able to offer anyone—that I know of. "When did you move here?"

"Last month," he says. "I'm subletting from my drummer's cousin."

The sound of pots and pans clinking in the kitchen tells me we're not alone, but I'm not surprised. Nick has always had roommates. He's painfully extroverted. Guy can't stand to be alone for more than five minutes but not in the clingy, obnoxious sort of way. More in the charismatic, life of the party, always down for a good time sort of way.

I follow Nick to the living room and he points to the middle cushion of a cognac leather sofa before slicking his palms together and pacing the small space.

"Nick." I laugh. "You're acting like a crazy person right now ... you know that, right?"

His ocean gaze lands on mine and he stops pacing for a moment. "I'm just so fucking nervous."

"You don't have to be nervous around me. Ever."

"This is different." He stops pacing for second. "This is something I've never told you before."

Oh, god.

My heart flutters and some long-buried hope makes its way out in the form of a smile on my face, but I bite it away.

I'd never admit this out loud, but last night a very real part of me believed this entire thing centered around Nick wanting to tell me he has feelings for me, that he wants to date me.

The idea is absurd, I know.

Things like this don't happen out of nowhere.

I'm not naïve and I'm not an idiot. I know the odds of my best friend going months without seeing me and suddenly professing his love for me are slim to none, but I've tried to come up with alternate theories and none of them made sense because Nick's never been nervous around me for *any* reason.

Ever.

What else could possibly make him nervous around me other than a heartfelt confession?

Crossing my legs and sitting up straight, I say, "Come on. Spit it out. I don't have all day."

He cups his hands over his nose and mouth, releasing a hard breath, and when he lets them fall, I find the dopiest grin on his face.

His eyes water like a teenage girl with a backstage pass to a Harry Styles concert.

Nick tries to speak but he can't.

Oh, my god.

He's doing it.

He's actually telling me he likes me ...

"Melrose," he says, pulling in a hard breath before dropping to his knees in front of me. He takes my hands in his and I swear my vision fades out for a second. "You know when we were kids and we used to tell each other everything?"

"Yeah ..."

"There was something I never told you," he says, eyes locked on mine. "I guess ... I guess I was afraid to say it out loud. I was afraid this thing I wanted so bad, this thing I wanted more than anything I'd ever wanted in my life, wasn't going to come true. And I thought that by admitting it, I was only going to jinx myself. So I kept it to myself, but I can't anymore. It's too big. It's eating away at me and it has been for *years*. But it's time. I have to tell you."

He's rambling.

Nick *never* rambles.

His trembling hands squeeze mine and then he rises, taking the spot on the couch beside me. Cupping my face in his hands, he offers a tepid smile that's soon eaten away by his own anxiety. "This is insane, Melrose. I can't believe I'm about to tell you this."

My mouth parts and I'm milliseconds from blurting out something along the lines of "I've liked you since we were kids, too ..." but I bite my tongue and let him go first.

"You know how I have my band, right?" he asks, referring to Melrose Nights, the band he founded in high school and named after *me*.

I nod, heart sinking. No ... *plummeting*.

"What about it?" I ask, blinking away the embarrassed burn in my eyes.

"My dream, Mel, was always to hit it big," he said. "Like, commercially big."

My brows lift. This is news to me. He was always about the indie scene, always so against the big music corporations that controlled every song the American people were played on the radio.

"Really?" I tuck my chin against my chest. "Because you always said—"

"I know what I always said," he cuts me off. "But the more I got to thinking about it, the more I thought ... I just want my songs to be in the ears of as many people as possible. And it's not even about becoming famous or having money, you know I'm not about any of that. I just want people to know my songs. That's all."

I swallow the lump in my throat and glance toward a wood burning fireplace in the corner where a crushed, empty can of Old Milwaukee—Nick's signature beverage of choice—rests on the mantle next to what appears to be a crumpled lace bra.

Guess he forgot a few things when he was straightening up ...

"Okay, so what are you trying to tell me?" I ask, squinting.

"We got signed ..." his mouth pulled so wide, he looks like a bona fide crazy person right now, "... *and* not only that, but we're going on tour with Maroon 5."

I try not to let my rampant disbelief show on my face,

but something tells me I'm failing miserably. He reads my expression, searching my eyes, and his silly grin fades.

"You hate Maroon 5," I say.

"I *used to* hate Maroon 5," he corrects me. "Anyway, the act they had fell through last minute, so they got us. We leave next week."

"Next week? For how long?"

"Six months." His calloused hands smack together. "Six months on the road with one of the biggest music acts in North America."

He says that last part out loud, like he's still in disbelief over this entire thing.

Which makes two of us.

"Wow, Nick ... that's ... this is huge. You were right. This is some big news," I say. Everything is sinking. My voice. My heart. My hope. "I'm so happy for you."

I throw my arms around him, inhale his musky scent, and squeeze him tight. There's a pang in my chest, a tightness in my middle, like that indescribable sensation that washes over you when you know something's about to change and things will never be the same again.

But I meant what I said. I *am* happy for him. I had no idea this is what he wanted, but now that he's shared this with me, I thrilled for him. He's my best friend, my oldest friend, and all I want is for him to be happy.

Plus, he deserves this.

Nick is insanely talented. Music. Lyrics. Singing. Playing. Producing. Mixing. It all comes natural to him. Keeping it under wraps on some lowdown indie scene would be doing a disservice to the rest of the world.

"I get that this is huge, Nick, but I'm curious ... why couldn't you tell me this over the phone?" I ask. "Why'd you make me drive all the way out here just so you could tell me in person?"

Nick leans back, studying my face as he rakes his palm along his five o'clock shadow. "Because I have a favor to ask you ..."

Lifting one brow, I study him right back. He's never asked me a single favor as long as I've known him (excluding those times he wanted me to talk to girls for him in middle school or steal him an extra Italian Ice at lunch).

"See, I'm taking over this guy's lease," he says. "I pay fifteen hundred a month for my half of the rent. Plus utilities. You know what a cheap bastard I am, right? I just don't want to throw that money away over the next several months and I don't want to stick Sutter with my half of the rent and everything because that's just shitty."

"Sutter?" I ask.

"Sutter Alcott. My roommate," he says. "Cool guy. Electrician. Owns his own company. You'll like him. Anyway, I know you're living in your Gram's guesthouse, but you're the only person I know who's not locked under a lease right now, so I thought *mayyyyybe* you might want to help me out for a few months? As a favor? And in return, I'll ... I don't know. I'll do something for you. What do you want? You want a backstage pass to a Maroon 5 concert? You want to meet Adam?"

"You're already on a first name basis with Adam Levine?" I ask, head cocked.

Nick smirks. "Not yet. But I will be."

"I don't know ..." I pull in a long, slow breath. "What about Murphy?"

"We've got a fenced in yard," he says, pointing toward the back of the house. "He'll love it here."

"What about your roommate? Would he be cool living with a stranger?" I ask.

"Totally."

"And you're sure he's not a serial killer?" I keep my voice low, leaning in.

Nick chokes on his spit. "Uh, yeah, no. He's not a serial killer. Lady killer? Sure. Serial killer. No way."

Our eyes hold and I silently straddle the line between staying put and saying yes to this little favor.

My cousin-slash-roommate, Maritza, recently moved out and got a place with her boyfriend, Isaiah, so it's just Murphy and I in the guesthouse now. It gets quiet sometimes. Lonely too. And Gram's on this travel-the-world kick lately. One week she's home, the next week she's in Bali for twelve days with her best friend, Constance or one of the Kennedys.

A change of scenery might be nice ...

"I'll do anything, Mel. Anything." He clasps his hands together and sticks out his bottom lip, brows raised.

Dork.

"Begging's not a good look for you. FYI," I say.

"Okay, then what's it going to take for you to say yes?" His hands drop to his lap.

I try to speak, but I don't know what to say.

"See," Nick says. "You don't even have a good reason to turn me down."

He's right.

I can't blame it on the location because it isn't out of the way. I can't blame it on my dog. I can't blame it on a lease. I can't blame it on money because fifteen hundred a month is exactly what Gram charges me for rent because free rides aren't a thing in the Claiborne family.

But aside from all of that, I know Nick would do this for me if I ever needed him to.

Shrugging, I look him in the eyes and smile. "Fine."

A second later, I'm captured in his embrace and he's squeezing me and bouncing like a hyper child. With one word, I've unearthed a side of Nick I never knew existed.

"I fucking love you, Mel," he says, hugging me tighter. "I love you so much."

I expected to hear those words today ... just didn't think I'd hear them in *this* context.

Chapter Two

Sutter

"You, uh, need some help with that?" I slam the door to my work truck and approach the blonde chick balancing a couple of tote bags on top of two giant Louis Vuitton suitcases as a little pug on a leash circles her feet.

I suppose it's in poor taste to decide you don't like someone before you even know them, but in the first five seconds of seeing my new roommate, I've already confirmed she's *exactly* what I expected—which is ... she's everything that's wrong with L.A. girls these days and *exactly* the kind of person I don't want to be shacking up with for the next six months.

For one, she's an "aspiring actress" according to Nick. That says it all right there.

For two, she comes from some famous family and me and the silver spooned types don't exactly mix.

And third? Who the fuck wears high heels to move?

Melrose tries to maneuver up the cracked walkway to my bungalow, stopping every few steps to rebalance everything. Her heels click along the pavement, her tits bouncing with each step, damn near spilling out of that tight white top of hers.

"Or you could just make two trips, you know," I say.

She stops and turns, following my voice, and then she pulls her oversized Chanel sunglasses down her nose as her hooded eyes narrow in my direction.

First impression? Hot as fuck.

Second impression? High maintenance as fuck.

Third impression? This is going to be a piece of cake.

When my original roommate, Hector, took a job across the country, he sent some guitar playing Casanova named Nick Camden to take his place.

All right. Fine. Whatever pays the rent.

But a few months later, Nick's band got signed to some bigtime record label and he got word they were going to be touring all over the country for the next half year. Nick, being the cheap ass that he is, wasted no time filling his spot with an old friend of his.

He assured me we'd get along, that she was "cool as fuck" and "laid back," and he promised me that if it didn't work out or if she decided to leave, he'd still pay his half of the rent each month.

One look at this piece of work and I can already tell we're going to lock horns like crazy. We'll probably spend the next couple of months going back and forth, bickering over who left the toilet seat up (wasn't me) or whose turn it is to wash the dishes in the sink (hers, naturally). And after a while, she'll pack up and go move back into her grandmother's Brentwood guesthouse and curse the day she met me.

I see no harm in helping speed the inevitable up a bit ...

I've been living with roommates for the better part of the last decade and I'm fresh off the heels of a long overdue breakup with a girl who put the "cling" in "clingy."

All I want is some goddamned breathing room and a little time to myself.

"Is Melrose your real name?" I ask, strutting toward her and grabbing one of her bags as I get a closer look. The scent of expensive perfume fills my lungs and I hope to God she's not as *extra* as she looks. "Or is it some stage name you made up to make yourself stand out?"

Her head tilts. "Sutter Alcott sounds like the name of an old, rich, white guy."

Touché.

I smirk, twirling my keys on my finger before finding the right one and shoving it in the lock on the front door. She stands behind me, waiting, and I'm sure I smell like ass. I've been running wires all day on some new build in Encino and it's been an unseasonably hot March.

All in a day's work.

We head in, and I place her bag to the left of the foyer, but this is where my assistance ends because I've got three priorities right now and three priorities only: a hot shower, a cold beer, and a juicy ribeye.

"You know where you're going?" I ask.

"He said it was upstairs. The bedroom on the left."

I chuckle. "Nick's a directionally challenged moron. *My* room is on the left. His—*yours*—is on the right."

It's odd imagining the two of them as friends, let alone *best* friends. He'll wear the same t-shirt three times before washing it and she's got on a pair of those red-bottomed heels I always see the women on Robertson wearing.

"You always dress up on moving day?" I ask, noting the curls in her shiny blonde hair and the coat of dark pink lipstick on her full mouth. I'm not sure if that's her God-given pout or if she's the product of some Kylie Jenner fad because it's impossible to tell in this town these days, but her lips are a work of fucking art, like two pillows shaped like a heart.

"I'm not dressed up." She peers down at her pointed heels before meeting my gaze. "*This* isn't dressed up."

Maybe where she comes from ...

"Ah, I see. So you just wanted to impress me then," I say.

Melrose's full, pink mouth shapes into a circle. "For your information, I had an audition today and I've spent all day driving all over town. I didn't have time to change."

"Nick said you were an actress," I say. He told me all about her and how he'd known her since they were kids and that her grandma was some award-winning movie star named Gloria Claiborne, which meant fuck-all to me. "But I haven't seen you in anything."

I'd remember a face like that.

I'd remember tits like that too.

Her pretty eyes narrow and she squares her shoulders with mine. "Can you please go longer than thirty seconds without underhandedly insulting me?"

"Is that what you think I'm doing?" I wrestle a smirk. I don't even know her but already I know I'm getting under her skin.

"Nick said you were cool," she says. "He didn't tell me you have the personality of an overconfident frat boy."

"Whoa, whoa, whoa. Now *that's* an insult." I place my

palm across my heart, pretending to be offended. "And can you blame the guy for overselling me? He's cheaper than dirt. He'd do anything to save a buck. I'm just glad I can finally get that Old Milwaukee piss-water out of my fridge."

Melrose glances down, like she's having a hard time comprehending that her lifelong bestie sold her out just to save a few grand. She releases the handle on her suitcase and folds her arms across her chest.

"He wouldn't put me in this position," she says. "He wouldn't ask me to live with someone if he thought we wouldn't get along."

"Maybe you don't know him as well as you thought you did?" I shrug, like it's not my problem and it isn't. "I've always gone by the assumption that everybody lies and everybody's in it for themselves. Life's much less disappointing that way."

"I don't lie."

"Bullshit," I cough. "Everybody lies. And if they say they don't, they're lying."

"I disagree but okay." She rolls her eyes at me and blows a breath between her lips. My gaze lingers on her distracting bee stung pout once more. Everything about her exterior is flawless—from her creamy complexion and curled lashes to her shiny blonde waves and tight little ass, and if I've learned anything in my ripe old age of twenty-eight, it's that perfect on the outside almost always equates to ugly, crazy, and dysfunctional on the inside.

I should know.

My last ex was the same way, just took a bit longer to crack through her ironclad veneer to get to the core of who she really was: an insecure, superficial Bel Air princess parading around like some vegan philanthropist with an organic vagina.

"Do you always have a giant stick up your ass or did I catch you on an off day?" I ask, genuinely curious but fully prepared not to give a fuck either way.

"What are doing?" Her brows meet and her dog paws at her leg. Clearly, he's over this conversation. "Are you testing my limits? Trying to feel me out? See how far you can push me before I push back?"

Close ... but not quite.

"I think I did the same thing once ... when I was a toddler," she adds.

"Ouch." I head to the stairs, feigning an emotional wound. "You done now? Can I go take my shower?"

"Just because I'm nice, doesn't mean I'm stupid. I read people, Sutter. And I can read you. I know exactly what you're trying to do and I highly advise you to stop."

I rub my hand across my chest, chuckling. "Is that supposed to scare me?"

Melrose's lips press into a hard line. "Nope. Just telling you to knock it off."

"Knock what off? Exact?"

"Whatever it is you're trying to do," she says. "Because I can promise you, it's not going to work on me. I have thick skin and patience for days."

I'm beginning to wonder if I underestimated her. All this time, I assumed she'd be some typical Brentwood Basic Bitch with zero personality, sky high ambition, and dungeon-level self-esteem.

But ... now I'm thinking there might be more to her than meets the eye.

"So ..." Her manicured brows rise and she steps toward me, squaring her body with mine, her posture mirroring the confidence of a queen. "How about we start over?"

"What?"

Extending her right hand, a slow smile claims her pretty face. "Hi, Sutter. I'm Melrose, your new roommate. It's so wonderful to meet you."

I don't know if she's trolling me or if she genuinely wants to start over—she could be acting for all I know, but I don't think that's how this works.

Regardless, I play along. I refuse to be bested at a game I personally started.

"Melrose, so lovely to meet you. Nicholas thinks the world of you. I'm sure I'll adore you just the same," I say in an over-the-top, saccharin sweet voice as I meet her hand with mine.

Two can play this game.

"Much better." She exhales as if she's partially satisfied before reaching toward a luggage handle.

I fully expected to meet a princess today, a junior Paris Hilton with an entitlement complex. What I got was a whip smart beauty who wasted no time putting me in my place.

And that's ... if I'm being completely honest with myself ... really fucking hot.

ACKNOWLEDGMENTS FOR WAR AND LOVE

This book would not have been possible if it weren't for the help of these amazing individuals. In no particular order ...

Louisa, the cover is beautiful! Thank you for never getting frustrated with me when I change my mind months after you've already sent me everything ... your patience and understanding is a godsend.

Ashley, thank you for beta reading, as always. I couldn't do this without you.

K, C, and M—hoes for life!

Wendy, thank you for being so easy to work with.

Neda, Rachel, and Liz, thank you for ALL the behind-the-scenes stuff you do. Your service is invaluable and you are a joy to work with!

Last, but not least, thank you to all the readers and bloggers and authors who share my releases, write reviews, or send sweet messages of encouragement. It's because of you that I get to live my dream, and I'm forever grateful for that.

ALSO BY WINTER RENSHAW

The Amato Brothers Series: Heartless

Reckless

Priceless

The Montgomery Brothers Duet

Dark Paradise

Dark Promises

Standalones

Vegas Baby

Cold Hearted

The Perfect Illusion

Country Nights

Absinthe

The Rebound

P.S. I Hate You

ABOUT THE AUTHOR

Wall Street Journal and #1 Amazon bestselling author Winter Renshaw is a bona fide daydream believer. She lives somewhere in the middle of the USA and can rarely be seen without her trusty Mead notebook and ultra-portable laptop. When she's not writing, she's living the American Dream with her husband, three kids, the laziest puggle this side of the Mississippi, and her ankle biting pug pup.

Winter also writes psychological suspense under the pseudonym, Minka Kent. Her first book, THE MEMORY WATCHER, has been optioned by NBC Universal.

Like Winter on Facebook.

Join the private mailing list.

Join Winter's Facebook reader group/discussion group/street team, CAMP WINTER.

4024

Made in the USA
Lexington, KY
06 July 2018